"Do you remember me?"

He'd felt sure she would recognize his face, even after all this time, and the last thing he'd ever want to do would be to frighten her. "I came here seven years ago. I had my… Well, I had two babies with me. My name is H—"

"I remember."

He stilled, letting her soft voice wash over him. Her tone was as gentle and patient as it had been that night.

"You asked me a question that night," he said. "You asked what mattered most to me."

Her gaze drifted lower, studying his lips intently as they moved.

"I didn't answer you then." He grimaced at the memory of the flawed, lost person he'd been years ago. "Because I didn't really know. But I do now. My sons matter most to me."

Her eyes met his again and her mouth tightened into a thin line. "Why now?"

"I was a different man then." He raised his chin. "But I've changed. I want to let you know who I am…"

April Arrington grew up in a small town and developed a love for books at an early age. Emotionally moving stories have always held a special place in her heart. April enjoys collecting pottery and soaking up the Georgia sun on her front porch.

Books by April Arrington

Love Inspired

A Haven for His Twins

Visit the Author Profile page at LoveInspired.com.

A Haven
for His Twins

April Arrington

LOVE INSPIRED
INSPIRATIONAL ROMANCE

LOVE INSPIRED®

INSPIRATIONAL ROMANCE

Recycling programs
for this product may
not exist in your area.

ISBN-13: 978-1-335-59827-1

A Haven for His Twins

Copyright © 2023 by April Standard

For questions and comments about the quality of this book, please contact us
at CustomerService@Harlequin.com.

Love Inspired
22 Adelaide St. West, 41st Floor
Toronto, Ontario M5H 4E3, Canada
www.LoveInspired.com

Printed in U.S.A.

And we know that all things work together for good to them that love God, to them who are the called according to his purpose.
—*Romans* 8:28

For Him. Thank You for giving me
a new purpose and a better life.

Chapter One

Holt Williams had never been a perfect man—most people would say he'd never even been a good one—but he was proud of having worked hard for seven long years to become a decent one. He was proud of having stuck it out. Of having resisted the tempting pull of the old life he'd led. But that warm swell of confidence in his chest vanished the moment the front door of the small cabin across the street opened.

A woman walked out onto the porch, leaned her left hip against the rustic porch rail in a graceful pose and sipped from a coffee mug she cradled between both hands. Auburn hair shining beneath the sun that slowly rose above the Blue Ridge Mountains, she made the perfect picture of cozy, rural contentment. The type of guilt-free, peaceful existence Holt hadn't experienced in years.

She lifted her head and fixed her gaze on the windshield of his truck, which was parked on the side of the dirt road in front of her cabin.

Inside the cab, Holt shifted uncomfortably in the driver's seat. She couldn't possibly see him. The windows were tinted and the pickup he drove now was a different make and model than the one he'd driven up her driveway seven years ago.

Still, his heart kicked against his ribs, and he curled his clammy palms tighter around the leather steering wheel. She'd met him back then—seven years ago, when he'd been twenty-nine years old and at his lowest. So low, his cheeks blazed even now with the memory of how he had approached her that night.

But the bright side was that she knew very little about him other than the fact that he'd been desperate at the time. And the kind, empathetic look in her eyes that night made him believe she might be inclined to forgive him and offer a second chance.

He held his breath as she continued staring, her eyes narrowed as though she saw past the thick tinted glass, recognized his features and read his expression. But after a moment her expression relaxed, and she returned inside, slowly pushing the door closed behind her.

Holt exhaled, ran his fingers through his

hair and smoothed his palm over his T-shirt, ensuring he looked presentable despite yesterday's long drive and a fitful night in a motel bed. It was time to face her; he couldn't put it off any longer. Not if he wanted to find his sons.

He exited the truck and strode slowly across the dirt road toward the cabin. Though it'd been seven years since he'd traversed the driveway to her home, his feet—and heart—remembered the path. Each painful step he'd taken toward her that night seven years ago had been imprinted into every cell of his being. He could still feel the warm weight of his infant sons in his arms, their wide eyes blinking up at him, their soft breaths seeming to beg him to reconsider.

His eyes burned, his step faltering. Spring rain had fallen for hours last night, and small muddy clods of Georgia clay coated the toes of his boots and sucked at his heels. The misty coolness of the morning air hit his bare forearms and he shivered slightly but pressed on, clenching his fists at his sides as he reached the steps leading to the cabin's front porch.

The same ornate hummingbird sculpture he recalled from seven years ago remained nailed to one of the thick columns at the top of the porch steps. *Hummingbird Haven*, the place was called, if he remembered correctly. He hadn't focused on the name the last time he'd visited...just the woman's face, her voice and the gentleness in her arms as she'd held his sons. He'd heard from locals she was exceptionally skilled at placing children in happy foster homes and that the cabins on her property served as the best shelter in the area.

He hadn't known what to say when he'd shown up at her door that night. Though he'd spent most of his adult years living a fast, carefree life on the rodeo circuit, enjoying days and nights filled with the sport, liquor and women, he'd slowed his pace when his sons were born, had given up the reckless excesses of the bachelor life he'd lived and tried his best to be a good father. Alone, ill equipped and inexperienced in childcare, it shouldn't have come as a surprise to him when he'd failed. But it had. And he'd never been more disappointed in himself.

It'd taken all the strength he'd had left to place his one-month-old sons in her arms that night and choke back the hot tears that had threatened to make him crumble. He'd wanted so much to gather his sons back against his chest, hug them close and leave again...even though he'd known he wasn't worthy of being their father.

She must've seen the desperation in his eyes and known how close he'd been to breaking down. She'd accepted his sons silently and taken them inside. Then she'd returned, had gently slid the straps of their diaper bags off his shoulders and asked one question. He hadn't been able to answer her, but instead of disdain, he'd only seen compassion in her eyes. For him—that night especially—she'd been nothing short of a hero and a better person than he'd ever been.

Now he hesitated, eyeing the hummingbird sculpture then the front door and large windows. The door stayed closed and the white lace curtains on each window remained still.

Unfurling one fist, he gripped the rustic porch rail and ascended the steps until he reached the front door. He knocked immediately, lifted his chin and straightened his six-foot-four-inch frame to its full height despite feeling smaller—and more unworthy—than he ever had.

Footsteps shuffled across the floor, a lock clicked as it released, then the door opened. And there she was—*Jessie Alden*. Three feet in front of him. Close enough to touch.

His memory of her—which had lingered in his mind for years—had been exact. Long auburn hair a unique shade of which he'd never seen before or since, dark brown eyes that could see right into the soul of a man and a curvy pink mouth made for smiling. Though Holt hadn't done anything worthy of earning her smile and hadn't had the good fortune of seeing it that night seven years ago.

She didn't smile now, either.

Instead, her mouth parted, and her eyes widened up at him, much in the same way as they had that night when he'd stood in front of her in the very same spot with two infants in his arms.

He focused on her eyes. "I have an answer to your question now." His voice sounded strained, even to his own ears. He cleared his throat and said in a steadier voice, "My sons matter most to me."

She frowned up at him but remained silent, her gaze pinned to his, emotions flickering through her expression, most too fast to identify save for one: *fear*.

He quickly took a step back. "Do you remember me?"

He'd felt sure she would recognize his face, even after all this time, and the last thing he'd ever want to do would be to frighten her. Though her reaction didn't surprise him—he was a big guy and his stature alone intimidated others more often than he liked. "I came here seven years ago. I had my… Well, I had two babies with me. My name is H—"

"I remember."

He stilled, letting her soft voice wash over him, pleased to discover he'd remembered the sound of it accurately over the years. Her tone was as gentle and patient as it had been that night. Forgiving, too? He hoped so. She was his only chance of discovering the whereabouts of his sons and, hopefully, reclaiming them.

"You asked me a question that night," he said. "You asked what mattered most to me."

Her gaze drifted lower, studying his lips intently as they moved.

"I didn't answer you then." He grimaced at the memory of the flawed, lost person he'd been years ago. "Because I didn't really know. But I do now. My sons matter most to me."

Her eyes met his again and her mouth tightened into a thin line. "Why now?"

Why not seven years ago? His cheeks burned. She hadn't said the words, but the question was right there in her defensive posture and guarded gaze. He didn't blame her for being suspicious of his presence…or less than welcoming.

He rubbed his hands over the jeans covering his thighs and ducked his head. "I was a different man then." He raised his head, met her eyes again. "My focus was on my own self-interests rather than my sons. But I've changed. I want to let you know who I am now, and I wanted to thank you in person. It wasn't something I thought I could do justice over the phone, but now that I'm here, 'thank you' doesn't do the job, either."

She returned his gaze, her posture relaxing just a bit.

"What you did that night—" he spread his hands, words escaping him "—taking in my sons and caring for them as you did. No criticism, no judgment. Not many people would do that."

She remained silent and still.

"I had no idea how to be a father." He studied her face, the flush blooming on her freckled cheeks. "Had no idea how to take care of them or what to do for them, and you…"

Throat tightening, he looked away and focused on a cedar tree at the end of the porch. He clenched his jaw and watched a branch dip in the breeze, dew sparkling in the morning sunlight.

"Anyway…" He withdrew an envelope from his back pocket, smoothed the slight bend in the middle, then offered it to her. "It's in here. What I wanted to say."

She looked at the envelope then slowly took it from him, her fingertips brushing his.

He flexed his hand, the warm softness of her touch still lingering on his skin. "I'd like to talk to you. To ask you a few questions about my sons if you'll allow me."

She stared down at the envelope she held for a few moments then looked up. "That's all you want? To ask questions?"

"Yes." To begin with, at least. He felt sure that was all she'd allow for now.

"I don't think..." She glanced over her shoulder then sighed. "Do you drink coffee?"

He smiled wide, hope swelling within him. "Yes."

"Then I guess you can come in for a cup." She stepped back, opened the door wider then hesitated, her voice firm. "But just one. I don't have time for more than that."

"I understand." He eased past her and entered the cabin. "Thank you."

The living room was small but cozy. A stone fireplace took center stage, a low fire crackling within, to stave off the slight morning chill, he assumed. One TV, two wooden end tables and a plush sofa and recliner in mismatched fabrics filled the rest of the room.

"Have a seat on the sofa. I just put a pot on." The clean scent of her hair—*sweet hon-*

eysuckle…or fresh apples?—hit his senses as she walked past him and left the room. "Won't take but a sec."

Holt glanced at the large sofa then crossed the room, his right knee bumping one of the end tables, rattling a delicate Tiffany-style lamp. He caught it with one shaky hand before it toppled over and steadied it back in position, unscathed. A relieved breath escaped him.

"It's okay." She'd returned, steam rising from a cup she held toward him. "That lamp's been broken twice before." Her lips twitched and a teasing light entered her dark eyes. "We managed to piece it back together both times."

"We?" His hand stopped in midair as he reached for the cup. "You and your husband?"

"No." The word was clipped. Her tone brisk. "Have a seat and ask your questions. I did tell you I didn't have much time."

Tensing at the abrupt change in her demeanor, he accepted the cup of coffee she thrust toward him then sat, sinking into the soft cushions of the sofa. She sat in the recliner facing him and he returned her stare for a few moments, a heavy silence falling between them.

Her eyes left his twice, veering off to a point high behind his right shoulder, and her fingers picked restlessly at the seam of her jeans along her thigh.

"Are my sons doing well?" he asked. "Are they safe and happy?"

She nodded but her expression remained stern.

Oh, man. Where to begin? His name, maybe? He'd known this task would be difficult, but he hadn't anticipated that the bright, revealing light of day and the knowing look in her eyes would be so intimidating. He leaned forward, propped his elbows on his knees and sipped from the cup, flinching as the bitter brew scalded his tongue.

Her face paled. "I'm sorry. It's too hot. Or maybe I should've added cream or sug—"

"It's okay. I normally take it black anyw—"

"But I didn't expect you to show up here, you know?" Her cheeks flushed a bright pink. "Right out of thin air." She snapped her fingers. "Just like that, after seven years."

"I know I should've called, but—"

"I never thought you'd come back. No one ever comes back."

"I realize my coming here is a shock, bu—"

"What is it you really want?"

He froze and searched her expression. Her gaze had moved beyond him again, past his right shoulder. Focused intently on that same spot. "I didn't come to upset you," he said softly.

Her eyes returned to his. "Then why? Why'd

you come?" Her tone hardened. "And tell me the truth. I've dealt with enough men like you to know you're withholding something."

"Men like me?" The judgmental grimness in her expression sent an unexpected ache through him. He set the coffee cup on the end table and stood, then spun away and strode around the couch, his gaze skimming the wall adorned with pictures in various styles of frames. "I'm not perfect, Jessie. Never claimed to be. But I'm not worthless."

He glanced over his shoulder at her. She sat on the edge of the recliner, her face paling again as she met his eyes.

"Do you understand?" His voice cracked and he turned away, his neck heating. "I'm not worthless…"

Holt stilled as his eyes focused on one framed photo. A large twelve-by-eighteen picture of Jessie in the most beautiful state he'd ever seen her: damp hair plastered in disarray to her sun-flushed cheeks, framing her bright smile as she knelt among smooth rocks in the shallow end of a mountain river. She hugged two boys—twins—their wet blond heads tucked beneath her chin. One boy hugged her back, smiling as he kissed her jaw; the other boy held up a flat black stone, laughing as he showed off his proud find.

The boys' features were familiar. Painfully so.

Holt tilted his head back, taking in the dozens of photos splayed across the wall in the shape of a tree with sprawling branches, each picture filled with the same boys at every age from bath time at infancy to blowing out candles at their seventh birthday party. And all of them included Jessie with the broadest, happiest of smiles.

"You kept them," he rasped. "You kept my sons."

"They're not yours."

Jessie closed her eyes, unable to believe the words had escaped her lips. What had she been thinking, inviting him in? From the moment she saw that truck parked across the road, she'd known something was up. She always kept a careful eye on who visited Hummingbird Haven to protect the privacy and safety of the troubled women and displaced children living at her shelter, and this morning an uneasy churn in her stomach had alerted her to the fact that something wasn't quite right.

But like that night seven years ago, the same pained, vulnerable look in Holt's hazel eyes as he'd stood outside her door had tugged at her heart and prompted her to lower her defenses.

"Those are my sons." Holt lifted one arm

and pointed at a recent photo of Cody and Devin that hung on the wall. "I'm a twin, myself. This could easily be a picture of me and my brother at that age. You don't think I'd recognize them?"

"I know you recognize them." Inhaling deeply, she placed the coffee cup she held on the end table and stood. "And I know how similar Cody and Devin look to you and your brother, Liam."

His eyes narrowed. "How do you know my brother? You don't even know me. All you know is that I dropped my sons off here seven years ago."

"I know your name is Holt Williams," she said. "It was on the birth certificates you packed in the diaper bags for the boys. Once I knew your name, it was easy to search for information about you. I always conduct research on the families of children who are left with me to better care for them and find the most suitable homes. Besides, you knew who I was when you came here. You knew my name, where I lived. You left two infants with me. It was only fair that I found out at least a little bit about you."

Holt frowned. "What else do you know?"

"That your father left your mother when you were eighteen to return to the rodeo circuit and that you went with him, competing as a bull rider." She eyed his muscular stature, clad in jeans, a white T-shirt and muddy boots. "Still do, from the looks of you. You won a couple championships six years ago, so there were several articles and interviews online. Most of them highlighted your career and how similar you were to your father when he'd competed at your age."

And that Holt shared his father's reputation as a fun-loving bachelor who partied hard, drank heavily, chased women and gambled on rodeo events, though that she wouldn't mention.

"There weren't many other biographical details except for one article I found," she said. "The journalist mentioned you'd been estranged from your mother and brother since you left home, but that you were a twin and he included a picture of you and your brother as kids." She glanced at the photo where he still pointed and managed a smile. "You both looked to be around the same age as Cody and Devin are in that picture. You and Liam are identical twins from what I could tell from your childhood photo."

He lowered his arm to his side, his jaw hardening. "Anything else?"

She studied his handsome features, the slight

stubble lining his angular jaw, his sculpted cheekbones and thick blond hair. Every inch of his impressive stature was that of the athletic, charismatic, carefree man the journalist had described in the article. The kind who chased every moment of fun in life and dodged all the consequences, abandoning any responsibilities.

"You say you've changed," she said softly, "but according to what I read in the article, you were what? Twenty-nine, seven years ago. You weren't a boy then. You were a man. A man who chose to abandon his own flesh and blood at a stranger's door."

He grimaced and looked past her out the large window by the front door, his hazel eyes wounded.

She ducked her head. "I... I'm sorry. That was unfair and wrong of me. I'm sure you did what you thought was best for Cody and Devin at the time. You protected them by doing the responsible thing and I'm glad you brought them here. More than that. I'll always be grateful to you for bringing them to me that night."

More than he'd ever know. Her attention strayed to the photo he'd noticed on the wall where Cody and Devin smiled as they hugged her in the river. A friend had taken that picture only a week ago on the same day she'd asked the boys how they felt about her adopting them. She'd been nervous about discussing the topic with Cody and Devin. She felt sure the boys would ask why she'd waited so long. Truth was, she'd held fast to a self-imposed rule to not get too emotionally attached to any resident at Hummingbird Haven since she'd opened the shelter over a decade ago. Her goal was to help abused women start a new life and place children in loving homes with supportive families—not create a family of her own.

But Cody and Devin had stolen her heart the moment they'd settled into her arms seven years ago, and she'd been unable to part with them since. Essentially, she'd served as Cody and Devin's mother from day one and as the years passed, adoption seemed like the natural, right thing to do.

Thirty-five years old now, she'd known ever since her teens that due to ovarian cysts and subsequent surgery she'd never be able to have children of her own. But Cody and Devin had changed that. They'd made her a mother in every sense of the word save for the legal technicality, and with the boys' blessing, she'd begun the process of achieving that as well.

"You don't know me as well as you think you do." Holt's hoarse voice pulled her eyes back to him. He still stared out the window, his broad shoulders lowered. "Where are my sons now?"

"They're at school," she said.

"I want to see them."

She shook her head. "That's out of the question."

He faced her then, a piercing look in his eyes. "Why?"

"I—It's been too long. Seven years." She spread her hands. "Legally, you have thirty days after leaving them to change your mind and regain custody. As it stands, they're settled with me. I applied for adoption recently."

One blond brow lifted, and his smooth lips curved humorlessly. "And you feel you have the final say in whether or not I have a role in their lives?"

She pulled back her shoulders and straightened to her full five-foot-six inches, resentful of still having to tilt her head back to look up at his face. "Yes. It would confuse them to meet with you now. Not to mention, possibly hurt them emotionally."

He remained silent for a moment then spoke again, his lips barely moving. "Why did you ask me that question that night—what matters most to me?"

Her brow furrowed at the abrupt change in subject. "I always ask that when someone abandons a child." She squeezed her palms together, her hands trembling at the painful memories of the various responses she'd received over the years. "I guess I hope that at some point, it'll help me understand why they chose to leave them behind." She jerked her thumb toward the front door. "Now, I appreciate your concern for Cody and Devin, but they're happily settled and it's time you left."

His gaze roved over her face and his mouth moved as though to speak but he seemed to think better of it and instead, he strode across the room and opened the door.

Pausing on the threshold, he looked back at her. "I'm sorry my returning is difficult for you, and the last thing I'd ever want to do is hurt Cody and Devin. But they *are* my sons, and I won't leave them again. My cell number is in the card I gave you and I'm staying at the Hope Springs Motel. I'd like the opportunity to explain myself and see my sons. Even if only from a distance."

Jessie clenched her teeth. "Please go. I don't understand why you think you can just waltz back into Cody and Devin's lives like this."

He did as she asked but before closing the door behind him, he said, "Because from what I remember of you that night and knowing what it is you do here, I hoped you believed in second chances."

Chapter Two

You don't know me as well as you think you do.

Jessie, standing at the kitchen island in her cabin, chopped a carrot into small slices then glanced at the envelope Holt had given her six hours earlier. There it sat on the kitchen island where she'd left it this morning, unopened and unread. She'd passed it a dozen times throughout the day as she'd loaded dirty dishes into the dishwasher, swept and mopped the kitchen floor and carried loads of laundry through the kitchen to the washer and dryer. Each time she'd passed the letter, her eyes had fixated on it, Holt's pained voice whispering through her mind.

I hoped you believed in second chances.

She tightened her grip on the knife she held, grabbed a cucumber from the pile of vegetables she'd placed on the kitchen island and chopped. That was the problem—she did. She absolutely did believe in second chances, and normally, she would be welcoming and receptive to any parent who returned to her door and inquired about their child—although that had never occurred before—and she should've extended the same welcome to Holt as well.

Only, offering Holt a second chance meant so much more than it would were she to extend the opportunity to someone else. Offering Holt a second chance meant more than just disrupting Cody and Devin's lives—though that was concerning enough. It also meant jeopardizing the future she was working so hard to secure for them. A future that included the long-awaited adoption that would legalize her as their mother.

And that realization alone—that she was placing her own selfish wishes above what might be best for Cody and Devin, and to some extent, even Holt—made her feel even guiltier than she already did for turning him away so quickly. After all, hadn't her mission at Hummingbird Haven always been to unite children with families who loved them rather than keep them apart?

Her head throbbed. She dropped the knife onto the counter, rubbed her temples then paced around the kitchen island. A queasy sensation filled her stomach as she recalled Holt's expression the night he'd left Cody and Devin in her care seven years ago. She'd had no doubts that he'd been desperate, frightened and exhausted. There had been tears in his eyes when he'd placed his sons in her arms, and he'd paused more than once as he'd walked back up her driveway toward his truck, glancing back at her cabin as though he'd changed his mind. But in the end, he hadn't returned. He'd hopped back in his truck, cranked the engine and driven off into the dark summer night without a word of explanation as to why he'd abandoned his sons.

Though…

Her steps slowed. Despite that, she had to admit he'd done the responsible thing and sought help. He'd brought Cody and Devin to a shelter where he knew they'd be taken care of properly and would hopefully be placed with a loving family. Holt had done exactly what she'd begged troubled mothers to do for years for their infants: bring them to safety rather than abandon them in an irresponsible manner.

How could she blame him for doing exactly as she hoped more troubled parents would? He'd done more for his sons than her own mother had done for her.

Jessie's steps halted. Her mother—whoever she was—had wrapped her, unwashed and only hours old from what Jessie had been told years later, in a blanket and left her on the paved ground of a motel parking lot. It'd been below freezing that night and only by God's grace had someone stumbled upon her in time. That was, after all, the reason she'd established Hummingbird Haven. She never wanted any child to suffer or feel unloved, lost, or neglected.

After being abandoned, she'd lived in foster care until she'd aged out at eighteen years old, worked odd jobs for seven years and saved every penny she earned to be able to afford the property Hummingbird Haven resided on now. The property itself had been a blessing from God. Eager to move and unload the land, the previous owner—recently widowed—had reduced the purchase price substantially once she learned of Jessie's plans for the shelter and donated a hefty sum to help Jessie with the initial costs of creating the shelter. It had taken three years to finish restoring six of the eight cabins on the lot, including the one she, Cody and Devin lived in now, and two more years to get the word out properly and collect enough donations, grants and financial aid to establish her shelter permanently as a secure, reliable safe haven.

She'd spent the past ten years using funds she'd raised—and continued to solicit—to care for abandoned children, place them in good homes and help abused women establish a new, safe life for themselves. And over those years, of all the people who had abandoned children at her door, the memory of Holt's expression of despair and regret had stayed with her the most.

But feeling guilty and regretful over leaving his sons didn't necessarily make him good father material, did it?

Sighing, Jessie picked up the envelope from the kitchen island. She slid her nail under the lip of the envelope and withdrew the card it contained. Colorful flowers adorned the front of the card but there were no factory-printed words inside, only a message scrawled in rough cursive as though penned by a masculine hand. She began reading.

Jessie,
I'll say right out that I'm not good at this. I'm not good at finding the right words to say what I mean, and I've never been good at trusting people enough to share what I think or feel. To be honest, I've never been the best at anything of significance in life so far, except finding ways

to hold on and endure pain without complaint. But because I've lived fast and hard, I've learned just about everything there is to know about people and this I know for sure.

There isn't anyone else like you. I've never met anyone filled with the kind of empathy and compassion you greeted me with the night I brought my sons to you. And I've never met anyone who would take in someone else's children without hesitation. I'm sure there are other people in the world with hearts as big as yours, but I've never met them. And I know from experience that they're hard to find.

Thank you for saving my sons. For finding them a home and security for seven years. For doing for them what I couldn't do at the time.

Now I'm asking for your help again. Please help me find my sons and get them back...because they are what matter most to me. I can answer your question now. I love my sons and I'm ready to be the father Cody and Devin deserve. The father I should've been years ago. I just need a second chance.

Sincerely,
Holt Williams

Jessie stared down at the card in her hands, blinking back tears. "Oh no. Oh no, not now. He can't be asking this of me now. Not when I'm about to become their mother." She dropped her head back and stared up at the exposed wooden beams that comprised the vaulted ceiling. "*You* can't be asking this of me. Not n—"

A horn blared outside.

"Great." Jessie wiped her eyes, stuffed the card in the waistband of her jeans and ran to the other side of the island. She swept the freshly chopped carrots and cucumbers into a large bowl and sealed the plastic lid on top. "Just great."

She was late. Holt had already disrupted the boys' carefully planned routine.

Jessie stacked another large plastic container she'd filled with pimento and cheese tea sandwiches on top of the vegetable bowl, scooped both up in her arms and race-walked outside onto the front porch just as a large multicolored van, painted with rainbows, hummingbirds and a large yellow sun, turned onto the driveway. Every window was open and six young faces smiled at her from the openings, hands waving and voices shouting in unison, "We're home, Jessie!"

"I missed you," Jessie shouted back, struggling to hold on to the plastic containers in her arms as she waved back with one hand.

The van rumbled past her cabin, turned left onto a dirt road and continued through a patch of thick forest toward the large Hummingbird Haven community building located several feet behind Jessie's cabin.

Clutching the food containers to her chest, Jessie hustled down her front steps and down the dirt path, following the van as it slowly maneuvered its way to the community building and parked beside the log structure. The doors opened and a young woman hopped out of the driver's seat, then assisted the six children as they all scrambled out of the van and walked into the community building save for two blond-headed boys who jogged over to Jessie, their backpacks jostling around on their backs.

"You're late." Devin, a seven-year-old with the shrewdness of an eighty-year-old man, propped his fists on his hips and narrowed his eyes up at her.

Jessie nodded. "I know."

"What's wrong?"

She summoned a smile. "Not a thing. I'm just running behind is all."

His hazel eyes—the same shade as Holt's—

narrowed even more on her face. "Really? You're okay?"

She smiled wider. So wide her cheeks hurt. "Really. I promise you I'm fine. There's nothing to worry about."

And there wasn't. Not really. She'd see to that. Devin had begun asking questions about his parents two years ago and she'd been as truthful as she could be without oversharing to the point of hurting him. But Devin was smart—gifted, even, if what his teachers suspected about his abilities turned out to be true. And he'd spent far more time than Cody over the past two years prodding her for information about his parents, wondering why they'd never been around and worrying about the future. She'd hoped initiating adoption proceedings would put his mind at ease. And it had, to a certain extent, but while Cody led with his heart, Devin led with his head, and easing Devin's worries about his and Cody's future had proven to be more difficult than she'd expected.

"Hey, Jessie." Cody, flashing his ever-present smile, hugged her waist and eyed the containers she held. "Peanut butter and jelly day?"

"'Fraid not." She bent and kissed his forehead. "You had that yesterday, and two days in a row is a bit too much sugar. Today is pimento and cheese day."

Cody groaned but asked hopefully, "Did you cut the crusts off?"

"Indeed."

Devin scooted close and peeked into the clear bowl she held in her arms. "Veggies, too?" He looked up at her and licked his lips. "Cucumber? And did you bring the ranch dressing?"

Grinning—sincerely this time—Jessie kissed his forehead, too. "Yep on both counts. I put a bottle of dressing on the table earlier and have an extra bottle at our cabin if needed, so you can glop on as much as you want." She glanced at Cody. "And I made chocolate milk to go with the mini sandwiches and veggies, so you'll still get a decent dose of sugar."

"Thanks, Jessie!" Both boys spoke in unison, hugged her waist one more time then darted inside the building.

Jessie laughed. Aside from video game hour, snack time was the boys' favorite part of the day, and though they were small, they put away enough sandwiches and salad every afternoon after school to feed two horses.

"Those two are gonna eat you out of house and home one day." Zoe Price, a vivacious and eternally optimistic twenty-nine-year-old who served as Jessie's assistant manager, grinned as she strolled over.

Jessie shrugged. "They're growing boys, and goodness knows they get their fair share of exercise the way they run around this place."

"Still…" Zoe lifted the lid on one container, slipped her hand inside and stole two tea sandwiches. "I hope you have enough."

Laughing, Jessie smacked her hand. "Get your grubby paw out of there."

"Hey," she muttered around a mouthful of pimento cheese, "I'm still growing, too." She giggled and motioned outward with her arms. "Just the wrong way."

Jessie laughed and shook her head. "Girl, I wish I had your metabolism." Not to mention Zoe's energy and athleticism. Zoe loved exploring the outdoors and her muscular physique showed it. "Why do you think I've cut back on making peanut butter and jelly sandwiches? I gain five pounds just smelling those things."

"Aw, hush up." Holding a tea sandwich in one hand, Zoe took the veggie container from Jessie's overloaded arms and walked with her toward the community building. "You're gorgeous and you know it."

Jessie smiled. "Oh, now I remember why I hired you."

"Because I give it to you straight." Zoe popped her last tea sandwich into her mouth, saying around a mouthful, "The good and the bad."

That was true. In the past five years Jessie had worked with her, Zoe had always been honest to a fault. She'd never held back her opinions—especially if they differed from Jessie's—and she'd always been equally eager to compromise. Their business partnership and close friendship had laid the foundation for a thriving and welcoming safe haven for everyone.

"Which," Zoe continued, "I think I should warn you that Devin had a rough day at school today."

Jessie frowned. "What happened?"

Zoe lowered her voice as they entered the community building. "The teacher told me she asked the class to write about what they planned to do over spring break next month. They were asked to read what they wrote to the class and when Marjorie Middleton stood up and read about going camping with her dad and how great he was—"

"Let me guess." Jessie winced. Marjorie Middleton had been Devin's nemesis since kindergarten when she'd beaten him in a relay race and given him a Valentine's card.

He couldn't stand that Marjorie was a faster runner than he was or her *ooey-gooey-girly stuff* as he'd put it, and Marjorie's tendency to wax poetic about her beloved father had only exacerbated their rift. "Devin had something negative to say."

"Yep," Zoe whispered as they approached the kids, who sat at one of several wooden tables laden with plates, cups, napkins and utensils. "He said dads were good for nothing and that moms do all the work anyway so who needed them? Then he refused to read what he wrote, balled up his paper and threw it in the trash."

"Oh no." Jessie set the tea sandwich container on the table and caught Devin's eye. She pointed to a seat at another table away from the other kids. Noticing the stern look on her face, he complied, blushing and ducking his head as he walked over to the table and had a seat.

"Here it is." Zoe set the salad on the table, withdrew a wrinkled piece of notebook paper from her pocket and pressed it into Jessie's hand. "I'll take care of snack time so y'all can have a talk. Go easy on him, okay?"

Jessie took the paper and nodded. Zoe had always had a soft spot for Devin.

"Now, then." Zoe clapped her hands and briskly rubbed them together. "I'm in charge of snack time while Jessie and Devin have some alone time, then we'll start on homework. Who wants to help me pour the chocolate milk?"

Tabitha, a thirteen-year-old who'd lived with her mother and younger sister at Hummingbird Haven for two months, volunteered, smiling shyly at Jessie as she passed her to join Zoe on the other side of the table. Her younger sister, Katie, sprang up and, sticking close to Tabitha's side, offered to help as well. They'd be missing their mother, Peggy Ann, by now. After escaping an abusive marriage, Peggy Ann had gotten her first job in fifteen years as a cashier at a local hardware store and wouldn't be home for another three hours.

Miles, a quiet five-year-old boy who'd arrived at Hummingbird Haven two weeks ago after being abandoned by his mother, smiled as Jessie walked by. Confused and frightened when he'd first arrived, he hadn't spoken or smiled for the first full week. He'd managed his first smile and words three days ago and seemed to be settling in but was still clearly uncomfortable. Which was to be expected.

Miles' mother, his only living relative, had packed her bags and left home early one morning with her boyfriend and didn't return. Miles, left alone in their apartment, had gone to a neighbor's house two days after his mother had left, seeking help and had eventually been placed at Hummingbird Haven. Miles struggled to trust others and, his sense of security having been shattered, feared being abandoned again.

Cody, seated next to Miles, smiled as Jessie walked by but his eyes kept veering toward Devin with a worried expression. He and Devin had been protective of each other from the very start, and he'd be worried for Devin now that he'd found himself in trouble. A pleading look of forgiveness entered Cody's eyes as though he hoped he could soften her up for Devin. She gave him a slight smile. No matter how close she'd grown to Cody and Devin over the years, they still craved reassurance on a frequent basis.

They all needed her, but Devin seemed to need her the most today.

"So…" Jessie sat in a chair opposite Devin at the otherwise empty table and spoke quietly. "I heard you had a rough day at school today."

He didn't answer, just crossed his arms on the table and lowered his chin onto the backs of his hands.

Jessie unfolded the paper Zoe had given her and narrowed her eyes, reading around the wrinkles creased into the page.

SPRING BREAK
by Devin Williams

Spring break will be great! Me and my brothur will have a real mom of our on. Jessie won't just be our fostur mom she will be our real mom. Forever. She told us so. And it's better than other kinds of moms because she choosed us. She gives us sanwitches and hugs and plays with us and takes care of us. She loves us. She loves us so much we don't need a dad and can be a family on our on. Just us three. Cody don't think so becuz he wants a dad. but I don't. Dads aren't good for nothing. I love Jessie and don't ever want a dad.

For the second time that day, Jessie blinked hard, holding back tears that gathered on her lashes.

"I didn't mean to make you cry." Devin lifted his head and looked at her. A wounded expression—startlingly the same one she'd seen on Holt's face earlier that day—appeared. "We don't need a dad, you know? Cody wants one but I don't. Not when I got you."

She folded the paper back up slowly. A deep ache spread through her chest at the pained tone of his voice. "You and Cody didn't mention this when we spoke about the adoption last week. Are you sure you don't want a dad, too, Devin? Even as a wish or for pretend, maybe? It's okay. You can tell me if you do."

He scowled and balled his fists on the table. "No. Not ever. I want you. Just you."

Laughter broke out across the room, and she glanced at the other table where Zoe did a silly dance and growled as she handed each child a tea sandwich. "Y'all better eat these up before I do. They're my favorite!"

As the kids dug into their snacks, Jessie faced Devin again. "Will you do me a favor, please?"

Devin nodded.

"Will you apologize to the teacher and Marjorie Middleton tomorrow at school for what you said in class?"

He frowned. "But—"

"Marjorie loves her dad as much as you love me and I'm sure what you said probably hurt her feelings. She deserves an apology."

"But she—"

"You wouldn't want someone to say something mean about me, would you?"

He sighed and shoved his hand through his blond hair. "No, ma'am."

"And you have a good heart." She reached out and smoothed his ruffled hair. "If you make a mistake, you want to fix it as best you can, don't you?"

He nodded. "Yes, ma'am. I'll apologize."

"Thank you." Jessie smiled. "Now, I guess you can rejoin the others. You're to eat your snack and do your homework right after."

"Yes, ma'am." He scrambled up from his chair and headed toward the other table.

"Devin?"

He stopped and faced her.

Jessie's smile wobbled. "I love you, too, you know?"

A wide grin broke out across Devin's face. He ran back, hugged her tight and whispered against her neck, "I know." Then he darted over to the children's table, sat beside Cody and dug into his pimento and cheese sandwich.

"I think we're gonna need another bottle of ranch dressing," Zoe called out as she upended and smacked an empty bottle over Devin's vegetables.

"I'll grab one from my place." Jessie stood and headed for the door. "Be back in a sec."

Once outside, she pulled Holt's card from her waistband. She held it in one hand and Devin's paper in the other, her gaze moving slowly from one to the other for a full minute. Then she tilted her head back and glared up at the clear blue sky.

"I get it," she whispered. "I hear loud and clear what You're asking of me. But I can't do it."

There were no sounds other than the pleasant chirp of birds and rustle of leaves from the slight afternoon breeze. No response—or rebuke—from heaven.

"I can't do it," she repeated, still staring at the sky. "You sent them to me, and You don't make mistakes. They're my sons now—mine. And not everyone truly deserves a second chance, do they?" She trembled, her voice strained as both the card and wrinkled paper crumpled beneath her rough grip. "I *won't* do it."

Chapter Three

❦

Holt pressed his cell phone closer to his ear, muted the TV and sat on the edge of the bed in his room at the Hope Springs Motel.

"It's been four days," he said, dragging his hand over his stubbled jaw. "I don't know why I even unpacked. Jessie made it clear she has no intention of contacting me and I haven't heard a word from her." There'd been no messages for him at the front desk and no missed calls on his cell. "And I can't very well go back to her place after she made it clear I was no longer welcome."

"She'll call." His brother Liam's voice sounded confident across the airwaves. "I know she will."

A humorless laugh escaped Holt's lips. "And what makes you so certain of that? You've never met her, and you didn't see her face.

I'm telling you she doesn't want me anywhere near Cody and Devin."

"I know she'll call," Liam stated firmly, "because this time is different. You're different. If she has only a fraction of the goodness you thought she had in her, she'll take a chance on you. You're worth taking a chance on, Holt."

He stilled, his throat closing as he watched the weatherman's mouth moving silently on the muted TV. The weatherman gestured toward a map behind him, pointing out temperatures in neighboring counties during the morning newscast. His hometown of Pine Creek was too small of a community to be recognized on the map and though it only took a four-hour drive to get there from Hope Springs, it felt as though home were a thousand miles away.

Liam's heavy sigh crossed the line. "I never told you that and I probably should've done so years ago. Then maybe we wouldn't have lost so much time."

Holt closed his eyes, a feeling of bittersweet gratitude washing over him. He hadn't expected that. He'd been estranged from his twin brother for most of his adult life—ever since their father had packed a bag and left Holt's mother to return to the rodeo circuit and hitch up with another woman… And Holt, having just turned eighteen at the time, had chosen to go with his father rather than stay at the family farm and help Liam and his mother fight foreclosure. At the time, Holt had been desperate for his father's approval and willing to sacrifice his relationship with his mother and brother for his attention. He'd followed his father's lead and severed ties with his mother and brother.

It'd taken one year for Holt to realize—and finally accept—that his father had intended to leave his entire family—not just his wife—and that Holt had become unwelcome baggage on the circuit. After embracing a new wife and new life, his father had little interest in nurturing a relationship with his son from a former marriage.

Hurt and angry, Holt had been too ashamed to return home to the mother and brother he felt he'd betrayed and had struck out on his own, touring the rodeo circuit solo rather than with his father. Success had come fast and fierce, along with the reckless excesses that were in abundance when traveling the circuit. Holt had abandoned his Christian principles and embraced his new life wholeheartedly to escape the pain of having a father who didn't love him and his guilt over abandoning his mother and brother. He'd thought he'd succeeded...until his sons had been conceived. He'd been unable to bring himself to return home and seek help from the family he'd betrayed and, as a result, had failed to support and provide for Cody and Devin.

After he'd left Cody and Devin with Jessie, the pain of abandoning his sons had been so great that touring the circuit no longer offered the comforting escape it once had. Eventually, after a lot of prayer, he'd chosen to face his fears, guilt and shame head-on and become the dependable brother, son, Christian—and hopefully, father—he should've been. To his surprise, upon his return home, his mother had accepted his apology and welcomed him with open arms and no resentment. His brother, however, hadn't been as forgiving. Though they'd begun patching things up five years ago, Holt knew Liam still needed more time before he fully trusted him again. Still, Liam had never thrown around compliments lightly and Holt doubted he'd start now.

"Thank you," Holt said. "That means a lot to me, especially knowing I still have a long way to go in proving my loyalty to you and Mom."

Liam was quiet for a moment then grunted. "You start getting all sentimental on me and I'll hang up. I mean it."

Holt chuckled. "One minute older than me and you still think that entitles you to boss me around. Put Mom on. I'm tired of talking to you, old man."

Liam laughed softly then a faint rustling crossed the line before his mom spoke.

"Jessie hasn't called?" Concern and worry flooded her tone.

"No, Mom. I was hoping that after our visit she might cool down and, well, it doesn't seem she's going to call."

"But…" He could picture her on the other end of the line, biting her lip and twirling a long strand of gray hair around her finger. "Liam says she'll call." Her tone firmed. "And if Liam says so, it's bound to happen."

Holt smiled. His mother, Gayle, had leaned hard on Liam since the day Holt and their father had left her eighteen years ago, and Liam had been the one to stay behind and revitalize the family farm that now served as a bed-and-breakfast in southern Georgia. Without Liam's dedication, hard work and willingness to remain at the family home and put his life on hold for Gayle, Pine Creek Farm would never have stayed afloat after Holt and his father had left, much less have rebounded to the thriving vacation attraction it had become. According to Gayle, whatever Liam said was the gospel truth.

"But if she doesn't call…" Gayle's confident

tone faltered. "Well, we'll just have to go another route, won't we?"

Holt grimaced. "This is my responsibility. I'll see it through in whatever way is best for Cody and Devin."

"I know you don't want to involve a third party," she continued gently, "but you may have to if you want to see Cody and Devin again. I'm sure Jessie is a nice woman—must be to have taken in Cody and Devin as she did—but you deserve a chance to see your sons, too." She sighed. "When the boys were born, you and I didn't have a relationship and you didn't feel you could come to me, so I wasn't able to help you. But now I can. Darlene Fulton from church gave me the name of a good lawyer who specializes in parental rights—"

"No." Holt softened his tone. "No, thank you, Mom. But I don't want to involve lawyers unless it's absolutely necessary. I want this to be as easy for Cody and Devin as I can possibly make it."

"Yes, bu—"

"Can you hold on a sec, Mom?" Holt tilted his head at the sound of footsteps and muted voices outside the window of his motel room. Instead of continuing down the breezeway as usual, the footsteps stopped outside the door of his room.

He stood, walked to the door and looked through the peephole. Jessie and a clerk he recognized from the reception desk stood on the other side of the closed door, talking softly.

Holt lifted the phone back to his ear, his heart pounding so loud he could hear it echoing through the cell phone. "Mom? Tell Liam he was wrong. Jessie didn't call."

She had shown up at his door.

"Wha—?"

"I'm sorry, I gotta go, Mom. I'll call y'all back."

Holt ended the call, shoved his phone into the pocket of his jeans and continued staring through the peephole.

"And you're sure this is it?" Jessie asked in a low voice.

The desk clerk nodded. "Holt Williams, room three nineteen. This is it. I can ring his room first if you'd like."

"No, thank you." She reached into her jeans pocket and withdrew what Holt suspected was a tip—or bribery—and pressed it into the desk clerk's hand. He smiled then walked away, whistling.

Jessie stared at the closed door, smoothed her hand over her bright auburn curls, raised her fist to knock—then froze. She shook her head, her long lashes fluttering over her dark brown eyes briefly, before she spun on her heel and turned away.

Holt's hand shot to the doorknob just as she spun back, her fist rising again hesitantly. He stopped, afraid to move for fear he'd startle her into bolting.

Keenly aware of the effort it must've taken for Jessie to bring herself to his door, he forced himself to remain motionless and whispered under his breath, "Come on, Jessie. Knock. Just once to meet me halfway. That's all I need."

And…she did. Her knuckles had barely tapped the door when he opened it in response. She stumbled back in surprise.

"Sorry," he said. "Didn't mean to startle you." He motioned toward the peephole. "I saw it was you."

She nodded, her gaze roving over him from head to toe, taking in every detail. "I came too early, I guess." Her cheeks flushed. "It's only seven thirty. I'm used to getting the boys up and off to school by seven. I didn't stop to think that you might not be up yet."

He shook his head as he rubbed his stubbled cheeks and jaw. "I've been up for a while." To be honest, he'd barely slept the past three nights. "Just haven't had a chance to shave." He stepped back and opened the door wide.

"Thank you for stopping by. Would you like to come in?"

She nodded again. "Yes, but…" Her eyes drifted from his face down to his chest, and her cheeks flushed a deeper shade of red. "W—would you please put on a shirt?"

He glanced down and realized—too late—that he had yet to fully dress for the day. Bare chested and shoeless was no way to greet a lady, especially one of Jessie's caliber. "Uh, yeah. Sorry. Just…" He held up a finger as he backed away. "One sec. Don't move, okay?"

He opened a dresser drawer, retrieved a T-shirt and yanked it over his head. Thrusting his fingers through his hair, he paused long enough to smooth the hem of his shirt over the waistband of his jeans and tug clean socks on his feet before he faced her again.

She stood on the opposite side of the room. Her gaze scanned the freshly made bed, his watch and wallet laid out neatly side by side on the nightstand and the partially opened door to the small bathroom he'd showered in a half hour ago. The spicy scent of his body wash still drifted on the humid air left behind from his hot shower.

Maybe he should open the window? Suggest relocating to the lobby? Any request from her would be welcome so long as he could entice her to stay and talk.

Her chest lifted on a deep inhale, and she pressed her lips together before saying, "You're very neat." She met his eyes. "I wasn't expecting that."

He shoved his hands into his pockets. "What were you expecting?"

"I don't know. That's why I came." She studied his expression, the wariness in hers receding slightly. "I wanted to get to know you better. Find out if you're trustworthy. It's my job to protect Cody and Devin."

Holt walked across the room, grabbed his wallet off the nightstand and held it out. "Here. Take a look around. I have no secrets—not anymore."

Her brows rose and she stared at the brown leather wallet in his hand then took it from him, carefully avoiding his fingers. She opened it slowly, lifted each slim compartment with one pink polished nail and tugged his license free.

"You're from Pine Creek?"

He nodded. "My family owns a farm there. They run a bed-and-breakfast."

Her brow creased. "Do they know about Cody and Devin?"

"Yes. But they didn't seven years ago."

She studied his license for another moment

then slid it back into the wallet and returned it to him.

"Please." Holt waved his arm toward the dresser at the front of the room. "Feel free to poke around. I've already unpacked. Everything I brought with me is either in that dresser or in the bathroom."

She frowned and fiddled with the collar of her T-shirt. Three small freckles were at the base of her throat, clustered together almost in the shape of a heart, drawing his eyes to the graceful curve to her neck.

He cleared his throat and glanced down at his socked feet. "Go ahead. I know you're looking out for my sons. No secrets, remember?"

Jessie hesitated, then did as he suggested. She pulled out each drawer of the dresser, sifted gently through his T-shirts, jeans and socks, but shut one drawer quickly when she encountered his boxers. Then she explored the bathroom, tugging back the shower curtain and eyeing the bottle of body wash and used bar of soap on the tub's ledge, and glanced at the shaving kit, toothbrush and toothpaste tube sitting on one side of the sink.

"You didn't bring much," she said softly.

"I don't need much," he said. "Just my sons." An awkward silence fell between them. He grinned, lifted his arms and teased, "I promise I don't pose a threat but if you feel the need to frisk me for weapons, please feel free to do that, too."

She smiled and her entire expression lit up, warm and affectionate. The sight made him catch his breath. "Well, I already know you're not hiding anything under that shirt." Her smile dimmed. "But you have a bit too much charm for my comfort. Do you drink?"

"Used to," he said. "Not anymore."

"Smoke?"

"Same."

"Where's their mother?"

His head jerked, the blunt question catching him off guard. A latent pain returned and flooded his chest. "Cheyenne left Cody and Devin two days after she gave birth to them. The pregnancy was unplanned, and she didn't want children." He met her eyes. "I wanted them, though. That's the reason she went through with the pregnancy."

"You..." She nibbled on her lower lip then continued. "I don't mean to pry even more, but it's necessary. You weren't married?"

"No." He released a heavy breath. "We didn't know each other well. We'd only met a few weeks before when I was in Arlington, Texas, touring the circuit. We spent a couple weeks together. Later, when I found out about the pregnancy, I proposed but she declined. She liked her life the way it was and wasn't ready for a family with a man she barely knew." He rubbed his stubbled cheeks with a shaky hand and cringed. "I led a different life back then. One I'm not proud of. And I surrounded myself with people who lived the same kind of life." Holding her gaze, he stepped closer. "You don't think I deserve another chance with Cody and Devin, do you?"

She returned his stare, sadness moving through her expression. "That's not my decision to make." She slipped her hand into her pocket and pulled out a folded piece of notebook paper. "I read your letter. It was very open and honest, and I thank you for that." She lifted the paper toward him. "This essay isn't quite as honest as your letter, but the truth is in there and I think it's only fair you know what you're up against."

He took the paper from her, opened it, and began reading.

SPRING BREAK
by Devin Williams

He turned his back to Jessie and his hands trembled harder as he read the words scribbled by a seven-year-old's hand—his son's hand.

Each word sent a stabbing pain through his chest and coaxed a fresh sheen of tears to his eyes.

"He's hurt," Jessie said gently at his back. "And very angry."

"He has every right to be." Holt faced her then, searching for a small trace of forgiveness and understanding in her eyes. The kind he imagined he glimpsed the night he brought his sons to her. "Do you think some mistakes can't be mended? That sometimes there's no way to set things right again even if you want to?"

"I don't know." She looked away briefly then peered up at him. "But I won't keep secrets from you, either. I'll be as honest with you as you've been with me. I don't want you to disrupt Cody and Devin's lives again after abandoning them for so long. I don't want you in their lives, period. Especially not when I'm about to adopt them." Her shoulders slumped and she rubbed her forehead. "But that's my selfish streak talking. And who am I to judge you?" She shook her head and walked to the door. "This isn't up to me. I just follow where I'm led."

He followed in her wake, his hand lifting in appeal. "Jessie—"

"Grab your wallet." She opened the door but stopped on the threshold and glanced at him over her shoulder. "You'll need your license to get in where I'm taking you."

"Where are we going?"

"Back to the beginning," she said softly. "Then I'll decide how—or if—we move forward from there."

Holt ignored the sting of pride at her commanding words, grabbed his wallet and clenched his jaw. "I'm willing to do whatever it takes."

Jessie eyed him again, her gaze drifting over him from the top of his head to the tips of his toes. "We'll see."

Chapter Four

Holt knew Jessie had decided to test him and he also knew he had to pass if he wanted to see his sons.

"You wanna tell me where we're headed now?" he asked, arranging his seat belt into a more comfortable position as he sat in the passenger seat of Jessie's SUV. She hadn't said a word since they left his motel room and driven off in her vehicle ten minutes earlier.

The morning sun broke fully over the horizon as Jessie drove up a steep mountain, its rays striking his eyes with bright heat. Wincing, he flipped the visor down. "I agreed to do this your way, but I'd like to prepare myself a little, at least."

Jessie stared at the road curving ahead, her eyes hidden behind sleek sunglasses. After easing past the bend and reaching the mountain's ascent, she glanced at him, the mirrored lenses of her sunglasses reflecting his image. "Did you feel prepared seven years ago when Cody and Devin were born?"

He shifted uncomfortably in his seat, hating the look of weak vulnerability appearing on his reflected expression in the lenses, but answered honestly. "No."

"Exactly. You walked away from them once and you could do it again." She faced the road again. "I think it's only fair that I have you test the waters first before I allow you to dive in."

A heavy breath escaped his lips. "A test it is, then." He pressed his palms tight against the rough denim covering his thighs and refused to rub the gnawing ache in his chest.

He could do this. No matter what she had planned. He had a lot of mistakes to make up for.

The SUV began its descent down the mountain and Holt's gut dipped with unease. He jerked his head to the side, peering down at the passing scenery.

Homes and businesses comprising the small community of Hope Springs dotted the undulating valley along the foothills of the Blue Ridge Mountains. Technically a part of the sprawling mountain town, the Hope Springs Motel where Holt had chosen to bed down resided several miles outside the densest part of Hope Springs city limits and provided a welcome respite from the prying eyes of locals. He'd been careful to steer clear of the downtown community during his stay.

As a bull rider, Holt had led a nomadic life for years. He'd roamed the back roads of the smallest of small towns and enjoyed the bustling sights, sounds and diversions of the biggest cities, but had never grown accustomed to being treated like an untrustworthy stranger.

Having grown up in Pine Creek—a small town where everyone knew each other and their life story, or a somewhat inaccurate version of it—he'd had the fortune of others knowing him and his family well. His mother's and brother's reputations as upstanding citizens had extended to him for a time...until he'd abandoned them with his father and then later, traveling the circuit, his own Christian principles. Guilt and shame had rooted so deeply inside him that he'd become a stranger even unto himself, and he'd remained one for years.

But things were different now, he reminded himself firmly, turning away from the imposing sight of the buildings comprising Hope Springs city limits. He was no longer a stranger to himself. Instead, he'd become the good man he should've always been and was, as Liam had said, worth taking a chance on. Surely with time, even Jessie would be able to see that.

"So tell me," he said. "If I fail to impress you, how prepared are you to turn me away? To keep two boys away from a father who is eager to provide for them and truly wants what's best for them? Especially when one—or both—of them are missing a father in their lives?" He cast Jessie a sidelong glance. A muscle ticked in her delicate jaw. "Would that sit well with your conscience?"

Her slim throat moved on a hard swallow. "I don't know." She slowed the SUV and palmed the steering wheel, turning into a parking lot. "Guess this will be a test for both of us."

Holt closed his eyes briefly then forced himself to study the imposing structure in front of them. The multifloored brick building with a U.S. flag flapping in the breeze high above a blue metal roof had a familiar look to it. A large sign stood tall at the front entrance of the sprawling building in front of them: Hope Springs Hospital.

Instantly, he recalled the hospital in Arlington, Texas, where Cody and Devin had been born seven years ago. He'd memorized every inch of the building—it had haunted him over the years—and the thought of it made him stiffen.

Cheyenne had called him the night she'd gone into labor, and having supported her through prenatal visits and birthing classes, he'd been at the ready. He'd picked her up at her friend's house in Arlington where she'd stayed for the duration of her pregnancy, then driven her to the hospital and spent hours pacing the halls and lobby until receiving the good news that the C-section had been a success and that both Cheyenne and the twins were doing well. He'd been invited to the nursery to visit his sons and when he saw Cody and Devin swaddled comfortably in their cribs, sucking their tiny thumbs, he'd stood outside the nursery window, cherishing the sight of their precious faces for over an hour. Alone. Every second of that hour, he'd never felt more proud, ashamed, or terrified in his life. The conflicting emotions had been so overwhelming, he'd almost walked away the night they were born, convinced Cody and Devin would be better off without an irresponsible man like him in their lives.

"Were you present when Cheyenne had Cody and Devin?"

Holt nodded. "I still toured the circuit but stuck close to Arlington where she was living and never stayed gone long." His muscles tightened as Jessie parked in front of the hospital. "She didn't want to hold them. Never even wanted to see them." He glanced at Jessie, a strange surge of empathy for Cheyenne welling inside him. Unlike him, she, at least, had had the courage to follow her convictions. "Cheyenne knew she wouldn't be the kind of mother Cody and Devin deserved, and she didn't want to get attached to them. She'd already made her decision to relinquish her rights and give them to me. I was surprised that she agreed to go through with the pregnancy at all."

"I'm grateful."

The firmness in Jessie's tone prompted him to scrutinize her expression, but the reflective lenses shielding her eyes hid so much.

"If she hadn't gone through with it," Jessie continued, "Cody and Devin wouldn't be here now."

Holt stilled. "No. They wouldn't."

Chances were, neither would he. He'd probably still be touring the circuit, lost and alone. Desperate for another round of violence in the arena, the angry jerk and kick of a bull beneath his body breaking off another chunk of bitterness, wringing free another painful regret. He wouldn't have looked back or slowed down, and commitment would've never taken root inside him. He would've continued to wander with no purpose and no obligations, serving himself instead of others. And he would never have returned to his mother and brother.

"Cody and Devin have so much to offer." Jessie tilted her head. "Other than providing material security and the title of father, what do you have to offer them?"

The question caught him by surprise. So much so, she'd already exited the SUV and shut the door before he managed to open his mouth in a weak attempt to answer.

She rapped the hood of the SUV with her knuckles, the sun glinting off her sleek sunglasses. "Let's go."

The walk across the parking lot and into the hospital was a quiet one, neither of them speaking. Holt shoved his hands into his pockets as they boarded an elevator and traveled to the top floor of the hospital, his elbow brushing hers as they stepped to one side and allowed others to exit on previous floors.

When the doors slid open at their destination, a nurse, seated at a wide desk across from the elevator, looked up from a desktop computer and smiled.

"Jessie. Right on time, as usual." The nurse stood, brushed her blond ponytail behind her shoulder and held out her hand. "I take it this is your guest."

Jessie nodded. "Holt, this is Sharon James, head of the Hope Springs Boarder Baby Unit."

Unease coiling inside him, Holt shook her hand but remained silent, unsure of what to say and even more uncomfortable with what might lay ahead.

"Welcome to our safe haven, Mr. Williams. If I could please see your state-issued identification?" Sharon's smile remained polite and impassive when he did as she asked, but skepticism lurked in the depths of her green eyes as she studied his driver's license then returned it to him. "Thank you." She pointed to a lengthy form fastened to a clipboard. "Please fill that out. When you're finished, I'll give you the grand tour then introduce you to our newest boarders."

Holt completed the form with his personal information, signed an agreement regarding rules, policies and procedures then joined Jessie, who spoke in a low tone to Sharon, at the entrance of a wide hallway. The conversation ended with his presence.

"I'll begin with an overview of the facilities, then I'll introduce you to one of our boarders." Sharon's guarded gaze swept over him as she waved a hand and walked down the hallway.

"Follow me, please. Feel free to ask questions at any time."

Holt joined her, glancing once behind him at Jessie, who stayed behind, watching him with a blank expression.

Sharon began the tour by describing the process by which they receive abandoned children. "Georgia law provides moms—" she winced and smiled apologetically "—or dads with thirty days to leave a child responsibly. At one time, our state was, I believe, second in the nation for discarded infants. The law allows for safe havens beyond solely hospitals. Fire stations, police stations and entities licensed and staffed with volunteers trained by the state, such as Jessie and Hummingbird Haven. They can also receive babies. But to avoid criminal charges, the parent must place the child in the safe care of a person when leaving them. In other words, they can't just leave the infant on a doorstep or in a chair in one of our waiting rooms unattended. The child must be left with a responsible party."

Pausing midstep, she glanced up at him. "As you did when you left your sons with Jessie. And because you did just that, I imagine you know most of what I've told you already. I suppose I should've thought of that before I gave you the full spiel."

"No, I…" He shrugged awkwardly. "I didn't know the technicalities at the time. I just knew I couldn't take care of them properly and that Hummingbird Haven was an option." Face heating, he rubbed the back of his neck. "My sons were born in Texas and I traveled for work and found reputable babysitters locally whenever I stopped in a new town. That's how I found out about Jessie." He forced a laugh. "I've always found motel desk clerks are great at knowing all the best secrets of a city. Anyway, I, uh… After my sons were born, I tried to make it work for a while but after three weeks on the road, struggling in motels, I could see it wasn't going to. I couldn't afford a down payment on an apartment or house without working, I couldn't work without hiring a babysitter and I couldn't save money when I had to pay babysitters. I didn't have experience with babies, had no idea how to take care of them effectively, and at the time, I barely had enough money in my pocket to keep a roof over our heads."

And, he thought ruefully, he'd been too ashamed and afraid to seek help from the mother and brother he'd betrayed and had been too enticed by his carefree, solo life on the circuit to take on the responsibilities of being a dad and raising two boys on his own. All mistakes he'd regretted ever since. Continuing with the status quo had been easy...but the thought of going back—of facing up to his failures—had been too painful and overwhelming.

Sharon nodded. "That's a prominent reason why some of our babies are left here. We've had many single mothers who live in poverty find themselves unable to provide for their babies or find reliable housing. Many times, they're also dealing with dangerous situations like homelessness or domestic violence, or they have no family to lean on. They love their children and want to protect them, so they rely on safe havens as a last resort out of desperation. That's one reason we've expanded our efforts over the past few years to include more preventative measures and provide support and resources early."

She continued down the hallway, opening the doors of two rooms, each nursery painted with bright colors, equipped with cribs and padded rocking chairs, and decorated with baby-friendly mobiles and toys. "Although we receive annual grants and financial aid from local businesses that keep us in operation, we also rely on donations and community volunteers to fund additional projects. Since Jessie joined our team and became our strongest advocate, we've been able to secure extra funds to renovate our nurseries." She smiled. "It's important for every child to feel comfortable, safe and secure while they're here. We want to nurture their minds and spirits as well as meet their physical needs for as long as they remain with us."

Holt eyed the small sheep, moon and stars dangling from a crib mobile and imagined a pudgy hand and tiny fingers, like those he remembered belonging to Cody and Devin as infants, reaching up to touch the plush figures. "How long do the babies stay?"

"Up to one year." Her smile faded. "Beyond that, we're unable to maintain ample space for new boarders. But we do our best to place each baby in a loving adoptive home as early as possible."

"And if no one adopts them?"

"We place them in a supportive foster home or safe haven licensed by the state where a foster parent will continue the work of finding an adoptive family best suited for the child."

Holt pulled his gaze away from the crib and met her eyes. "Like Jessie?"

Sharon's expression softened. "Yes. She's been a lifesaver for many children over the years." She looked at the empty crib across the room. "Literally. Without Jessie and the hard work she does at Hummingbird Haven, many more children would be lost, as well as the desperate, abused women who need her."

"I can't take all the credit."

Holt spun around and found Jessie standing behind Sharon. Her expression remained inscrutable, but the tight line of her mouth had gentled.

"I've had a ton of help," she added. "Sharon and her team here at Hope Springs Hospital and my assistant manager, Zoe, have taken on as much—if not more—than I have. We work to build strong relationships with the community as a team and are stronger as a result. I suppose that's how the desk clerk at the Hope Springs Motel was able to direct you to Hummingbird Haven." Her head dipped briefly. "And why he was willing to lead me to your room this morning. We're a small community and don't forget strangers who wander through."

Holt stiffened.

"Well, now that you've been given the tour," Sharon said, "there's one last stop to make." She eased past Holt, farther down the hall, opened a door and swept an arm toward the inside of the room. "After you."

Holt hesitated then entered the room, the soft scent of baby powder and fabric softener settling around him. A discontented cry and shuffling sounds emerged from a crib on the other side of the room.

"Baby Ava's our newest boarder," Sharon said, walking over to the crib. "She's only been with us for two weeks but even though she's only one month old, she's an old soul and we feel like we've known her forever." A wail broke out as Sharon smiled down into the crib and she murmured soothing words before briskly walking toward the door. "I'll bring her tray and leave you to it."

Leave him to what? Holt stared at the small pink bundle wiggling and wailing in the crib, his gut hollowing.

"It's time for Ava's feeding." Jessie, standing by the door, gestured toward the rocking chair beside the crib. "Have a seat. You're her caretaker this morning."

"I'm what?" His voice caught. The weak, high-pitched tone of his words made him flinch. He looked down and flexed his hands, noting the thick calluses coating his fingers. Hands like his—big, rough and commanding on the back of a bull—had no place near an infant's delicate skin or fragile limbs. He'd never grown comfortable holding Cody and Devin during his brief time with them and had struggled with the awkwardness of it. "I…thought this was just a tour."

Brows lifting, Jessie leaned back against the doorjamb and crossed her arms. "Is that what you thought your return into Cody and Devin's lives would be? Just a tour? A hands-off spectatorship?" Her lip curled as her voice rose over the crying of the infant in the crib. "You're used to performing, right? Center stage on the circuit? All bravado and swagger? If you can't handle this, you can't handle Cody and Devin."

The rebuke in her big brown eyes pierced his skin and dove deeper into his conscience than he'd anticipated. One thing he'd learned in his short time with Jessie thus far, was that she was honest. Bluntly so. And honesty had been a rarity in his life for years.

"No," he said softly, the word lost amid the increasing wails of the baby. "That's not what I thought." He walked across the room and sat in the rocking chair. The arms were narrow and the pink pillow lining the seat thick, forcing him to squirm for a moment or two before he was able to settle into the constraints of the chair. "Okay. What do I do?"

She frowned. "What do you mean, what do you do? You fed Cody and Devin when you had them."

He cleared his throat. "Yes." He dragged his clammy palms across the rough denim covering his thighs. "But I was never very good at it." His face flamed. "I used to prop them up on pillows on the motel bed with one hand, sit in a chair by the bed and feed them with the other hand." He forced himself to look up at her. "I was afraid to hold them most of the time."

Jessie moved to speak but closed her mouth when Sharon returned, tray in hand.

"Her bottle is warm and ready to go," Sharon said, setting the tray on a small table beside the rocking chair. "Burping cloths are here, too. If you need anything else—" she pointed to a phone on the wall "—just give me a ring."

After she left, Jessie uncrossed her arms, pushed off the doorjamb and walked over to his side. "Are you right-or left-handed?"

"Right."

She picked up a soft white cloth off the tray and tossed it onto his lap. "That goes over your shoulder—your left will probably be most comfortable—but you can switch up if you need to. You'll want to settle her in the fold of your left arm and give her the bottle with your right." She hesitated, her tone gentle. "She won't bite, you know." A small grin teased her lips when he glanced up at her. "Well...she can, but it won't hurt." She smiled and tapped her fingernail against her straight teeth. "Not until she gets these, at least."

Surprisingly, a smile crept across his own lips. He exhaled and turned his hands over, palms up. "All right. I'm ready."

She moved to the crib, bent and lifted the pink bundle into her arms. A tiny pair of feet kicked free of the pink swaddling blanket and miniature fingers flailed in the air.

"It's okay, sweetheart. Breakfast is on the way." Jessie's soothing tone drew close as she lowered the baby onto his arms. "Keep her head cradled in the crook of your elbow and lift her head slightly." She pressed a bottle into his free hand. "Go ahead and offer it. She knows what to do."

One of Jessie's long red curls tickled his cheek as she straightened. He wiggled his mouth to ease the itch and focused on the warm weight of the bundle in his arms. She was small. So small, if he closed his eyes, he'd doubt she was even there…if not for the disgruntled cries filling the small room.

Hand shaking, he moved the bottle close to the baby's thrashing head. The nipple brushed her open mouth then her lips latched on, her body stilling and cries quieting.

"There," Jessie said. "That's better."

Holt stared. The baby's eyes, wide and blue, focused on his, a slow, occasional blink of her thick lashes the only interruption of her scrutiny. Her hungry sighs and rhythmic pull on the bottle in his hand tugged at something deep in his chest. Cracked the tall walls surrounding his heart and freed a fresh, overwhelming surge of pain.

"Ava," he whispered. An innocent child as young as Cody and Devin had been years ago. An infant someone had left behind, weak and alone. Vulnerable to the whims of those surrounding her.

Ava continued studying him. Her clear gaze moved over his forehead, nose, mouth and chin, then returned to his eyes again. A questioning look entered her expression, and he could only imagine how he must appear to her: rough, imposing and unfamiliar. A stranger.

Despair surged through his veins, hollowed his gut and weakened his frame. It slinked deep into his being and began rooting itself in his body, mind and soul, conjuring up all his fears of inadequacy as a father from seven years ago to the point that he wondered if he could even trust himself or his own intentions. He could feel doubt taking hold of him now, capitalizing on his guilt and insecurity.

His hand trembled and his fingers shook

around the bottle, dislodging the nipple from Ava's mouth. Her expression contorted, intensifying with fear and distrust, and she reared away, her cries echoing sharply against the nursery walls as she refused his clumsy offers of the bottle.

Wet heat filled Holt's eyes and coated his lower lashes. "She doesn't trust me."

"And once they know who you are," Jessie said softly, "neither will Cody and Devin."

Chapter Five

Jessie had lied to Holt—and herself—and she'd never felt like a bigger heel in her life.

The drive from the Hope Springs Hospital back to the motel seemed ten times longer to her than it had when she'd first undertaken it two hours before. Jessie glanced at Holt, who sat silently in the passenger seat.

Earlier, when Ava had grown uncomfortable in his arms as he'd fed her in the nursery, he'd ducked his head, and the moment they'd settled back into the SUV, he'd turned his face away and stared intently out the passenger window, his strong shoulders slumped and big fists curled tightly around the edge of his seat. Since she'd driven out of the hospital parking lot ten minutes ago, he hadn't spoken and neither had she, but a subtle glance confirmed what she'd suspected. Afternoon sunlight, spearing through the windshield as the SUV ascended a mountain, glinted off moisture trailing down Holt's stubbled cheek and jaw.

"I'm sorry."

His left shoulder lifted, and he dipped his head to the side, subtly rubbing his wet cheek on the sleeve of his T-shirt. "For what?"

His deep voice sounded strained, and his expression of grief lent him a less intimidating, vulnerable air. It was an odd sight, seeing a big, seemingly unbreakable man like Holt crumpling with pain.

An unexpected urge unfurled inside her, beckoning her to place a comforting hand over his or sift her fingers through his thick hair in a consoling gesture.

She squirmed in her seat then readjusted her grip on the steering wheel. "I'm sorry for judging you. I said I wouldn't, and I had good intentions but…"

It'd been too easy to let her residual anger and resentment over his reappearance in Cody and Devin's lives to resurface, especially after she'd placed Ava in his strong arms. After all, Cody and Devin had been nestled there once, seven years ago, and a part of her still believed that Holt—no matter what his circumstances— had been strong enough to make it work back then if he'd truly wanted to keep his sons. Instead, he'd chosen not to commit—just like her own mother had. Either that, or he'd simply decided to leave the hard work of raising them to someone else until it became easier and more convenient for him to assume his role as father.

She winced. There she went again, judging and blaming. Something she had no right to do. Especially if her prejudice cost Cody and Devin a chance to meet and possibly form some sort of bond with their father.

"I took you to the Boarder Baby Unit because I wanted to see if you'd shy away from holding Ava," she continued quietly. "If you'd be intimidated and tempted to walk away at the first sign of discomfort. To reconnect with your sons, you'll have to set aside your own needs and comfort in favor of Cody and Devin's. There's so much potential for this to backfire. Not just on Cody and Devin—but on you as well." She bit her lip. "But worse… I wanted to make you feel guilty for leaving them."

He nodded, still staring at the road ahead. "You succeeded."

"That was wrong of me," she said quietly. "You made a responsible choice to place them in someone else's care and I had no right to judge you for it. For Cody and Devin's sake, I should be finding a way to help you right now not hinder you."

The flashing Hope Springs Motel sign emerged over the curve of the mountain. Jessie slowed the SUV and made the turn, eased the vehicle to a stop in front of Holt's room, then cut the engine.

Holt unsnapped his seat belt, thrust open the passenger door and exited.

"Holt."

He paused, one hand on the door frame, face turned away.

"Give me a name." She leaned toward him and placed her palm on the passenger seat, the warmth he'd left behind seeping into her skin. "Not family, but someone who knew you seven years ago and still knows you now. Someone who can vouch for you."

His jaw clenched and he didn't respond.

"Please." She reached for his arm, but the distance was too great, and her upturned palm hovered helplessly in the still air between them. "I'm trying to do the right thing. I'm trying to give you a chance."

He faced her then, studied her hand then her expression, his eyes finally meeting hers.

After a few moments, he withdrew his wallet from his back pocket, tore a crumpled receipt in half then held out his hand, upturned beside her own. She grabbed a pen from the glove compartment and handed it over, watching as he wrote on the small scrap of paper in his hand.

When he finished, he handed it to her wordlessly, shut the passenger door then ambled up to his motel room and went inside, closing the door behind him.

Sighing, Jessie placed the piece of paper on her thigh, grabbed her purse from the backseat, pulled out her phone and dialed the number Holt had scrawled.

It rang several times before a gruff male voice answered. "Yeah?"

Jessie narrowed her eyes, read Holt's writing, then licked her lips nervously. "Is this Ty Branton?"

Something rustled in the background. "Well, now, that depends on who this is." He sniffed, a hint of amusement creeping into his tone. "See, you called me. So you gotta gimme your name first, baby."

Tensing, Jessie rolled her eyes. This did not bode well. "This is Jessie Alden. I'm calling on Holt Williams's behalf for a recommendation of sorts. Do you have a moment to speak with me? Answer a few questions about his background?"

Silence settled across the line then more rustling. "Uh…yeah. I'm guessing this is about his boys?"

"Yes. You mind if I switch to video?" In her experience, eyes were much more expressive than tone.

Squeaks, a thud then a heavy sigh. "Sure. Go ahead."

Jessie switched the call to video chat, propped the phone on the dash and eyed the middle-aged man who appeared on the screen. Mussed brown hair standing up in tufts, strong stubbled jaw and drowsy blue eyes faced her. He was in the act of lighting a cigarette, his blunt thumb flicking a lighter as he sat on the edge of a bed.

"I apologize for disturbing you, but I need some information regarding Holt's character and it's a bit time sensitive."

"Not a problem." Cigarette lit, he drew deep from it then blew out a thick cloud of smoke. "Jessie, was it?"

She frowned but nodded.

Ty sat up straight and presented a polite, professional smile, which she suspected he reserved for rare formal occasions. "Had a late night, so today's a late start, is all."

Don't judge, Jessie, she admonished herself silently. *And keep your opinions to yourself.*

She looked down and squeezed her hands

together in her lap. "Thank you for taking my call."

He shrugged. "Anything for Holt."

"How long have you known him?"

"Oh, about sixteen, seventeen years, I guess. Met him on the circuit when we were both nineteen."

"The circuit?"

"Rodeo." He smiled, a crooked—almost cocky—one this time. "Bull riding. We were both touring solo, going for broke at the time. He'd just parted ways with his dad and was competing alone. Never seen someone ride like Holt. No nerves, no fear. Just angry heat. A born performer. Night I met him, he owned that bull he rode and the arena. Crowd lit up like dynamite when he walked in." He chuckled then took another drag from his cigarette. "I was eager to learn from him, so I sought him out after, asked if he was interested in giving me a few pointers. Suggested we pool resources—I had a top-notch truck and trailer, his rusty pickup would barely crank at the time—and he took me up on it."

"How long did you two travel together?"

"Oh, years." His smile widened. "Two rascals running the road, catching winks between competitions in the cab of a truck day in and day out, you get to know someone real well.

Holt partied hard, but he worked hard, too. Always pulled his weight and then some. If he said he was gonna do something, he did it. I never questioned his word. Never had a reason to. It was tough making ends meet, but we had good times. Great times, really. We were like brothers."

The nostalgic—almost boyish—gleam in Ty's eyes made Jessie smile, too. "So you knew him well."

"Inside and out." His smile fell. "Back then, at least."

His gaze strayed from hers, moving off to the side, staring into the distance as he frowned.

"And now?" Jessie asked.

Ty blinked. Refocused on her. "Now?" He shook his head as he stubbed his cigarette out in an ashtray on the bedside table. "That's the thing. We parted ways when his sons were born. He said he wanted to raise 'em different than how we were living. Then, a couple months later he turned up alone, we partnered again and picked back up where we left off. But…things weren't the same. *He* wasn't the same. He worked but didn't play. Kept to himself and wasn't easygoing like he used to be." The corner of his mouth lifted in a rueful grin. "He missed them boys. Never got over leavin' 'em. He left the circuit again a couple years later to go back home to his mom and brother and start fresh. Said he felt like God was calling him in another direction. I've never been a religious man, so I didn't really understand it. All I knew was he was taking off on me again. I didn't give him a very good send-off, you know? We've only seen each other once since then, but he kept in touch over the phone pretty regular-like. Only, it didn't sound like him anymore. Still doesn't."

Jessie waited, her heart thumping rapidly in her chest.

"What I mean is…" Ty scooted to the very edge of the bed, closer to the phone's screen. "Holt's changed so much since he left the circuit that if I ran across him now…" He spread his hands, searching for the right words. "You know? Passed him on the street? I don't think I'd know him. Wouldn't recognize him even. That's how much he feels like a stranger to me now."

Jessie's mouth parted soundlessly. She cleared her throat and tried again. "A stranger?"

"Yeah." Ty nodded several times, mulling it over. "That's the best I can describe it." His grin returned as he gestured toward his rumpled hair and wrinkled T-shirt. "Now, I ain't much to look at right this moment, and no one in their right mind would say I'm anyone to be—" he made air quotes with his fingers "—recommending somebody for something. But honestly, Holt loves those boys something fierce. And though he and I live different kinds of lives now, he ain't never looked down on me. He checks in on me from time to time, sees if I need anything. Who he is now...well, he's the kind of man I wish I could be."

Jessie studied his expression, the wistful admiration in it warming her chest.

"Well..." He cocked his head to the side and wrinkled his nose, his boyish grin returning. "To be fair, I only wish for it Monday through Thursday. The weekends are too much fun for me to trade for that strait-laced life Holt's living nowadays."

Laughter burst from Jessie's lips. "A strait-laced life can be fun, too, Ty."

"With you?" He chuckled. "I bet."

Jessie's face flamed.

"Forgive me." He winked. "Old habits die hard. Anyways, I hate to cut short time with a gorgeous woman, but I gotta compete tonight and I need my beauty rest. Anything else you wanna know?"

She shook her head. "That's all I need. Thank you for taking my call."

He grinned. "You bet. Give Holt a shout for me."

Ty's image disappeared and a message popped up, noting he'd ended the call.

Jessie removed her cell phone from the dash, tossed it back into her purse and stared at the closed door of Holt's motel room.

Said he felt like God was calling him in another direction.

He feels like a stranger to me now.

"A stranger," she whispered.

According to Ty, Holt *had* changed over the years. And if she decided to give Holt a chance with Cody and Devin, a stranger might be exactly what Holt needed to be.

"Say what?"

Zoe sat in a rocking chair on the front porch of Jessie's cabin, a homemade bacon, egg and cheese biscuit in one hand, except for one big bite half-chewed in her open mouth, and a mug full of hot coffee in the other hand. An expression of horrified disbelief enveloped her face.

"An unpaid handym—" Voice catching on a bit of unchewed biscuit, Zoe closed her mouth long enough to fully chew and swallow, then continued. "You say you intend to hire a handyman who'll work for no pay?" Her brows rose. "I've searched for months for someone to accept the wage we can actually afford to pay and there've been no takers. Do you seriously think you're going to find someone who wants to work without being paid at all? Especially in this economy?"

Jessie rocked back in her own rocking chair and tried to adopt a neutral expression. "I've already found one." She sipped coffee from the mug she held, hiding her eyes behind the rim of the cup. "Or may have found one. He's on his way here now. He's keen on sticking around town for a while, so I thought he might agree to volunteer. I called him this morning, told him to pack his bags and come around. That I had a proposition for him. And I wanted you to meet him, take a good look at him and let me know if you approved of him staying on the property."

After her video chat with Ty yesterday afternoon, she'd driven home and gone about the regular duties of the day—laundry, cleaning cabins, yard work, cooking supper and spending time with the boys after school—but she'd been unable to think of little else but Holt.

The regrets in his eyes and tears on his face as they'd driven away from Hope Springs Hospital yesterday had stayed with her throughout the night and into the first light of morning. Holt wasn't a perfect person, but who was? And according to Ty, he had changed.

But exactly how much had he changed? And what risks would she be allowing into Cody and Devin's lives if she introduced Holt to them? Those were the worries that still irked her conscience.

Zoe's eyes widened. "Who is he?"

Jessie stared down at her coffee and watched a lone dreg float aimlessly across the brown liquid. "He's staying at the Hope Springs Motel."

A hint of suspicion crossed Zoe's expression. "I didn't ask where he's staying. I asked who he was."

"I know." Jessie rocked her chair faster, placing one hand on the untouched bacon, egg and cheese biscuit on her lap to prevent it from sliding off. "Just thought I'd give you some context is all."

Zoe frowned, a bit of egg dangling from her lower lip as she looked from Jessie's face to the biscuit in her hand then back. "You're trying to butter me up, aren't you? That's why you made me your famous biscuits, fresh-brewed coffee and rolled out the red porch carpet when I got back from dropping the kids off at school."

Jessie took another sip of coffee to hide her smile. She was indeed guilty of all Zoe accused. "Maybe." She glanced up and met Zoe's eyes. "I need your advice."

"That's always available to you." Zoe set her half-eaten biscuit and coffee mug on the porch rail, wiped her mouth with a napkin then crossed her arms. "But you've got to be honest with me."

Jessie closed her eyes and pinched the bridge of her nose. "I know." Opening her eyes, she met Zoe's gaze again. "His name's Holt Williams."

"Holt Will…" Zoe's gaze veered away as she mulled over the name, then her eyes, full of surprise, met Jessie's again. "Holt Williams? As in Cody and Devin's Holt?"

"He's not Cody and Devin's," Jessie stated firmly. "And Cody and Devin are definitely not his."

"Oh, but they are." Zoe leaned closer and frowned. "We are talking about the same Holt Williams here, right? Cody and Devin's biological father?"

"Yes."

"Is this a joke?"

"No."

Zoe froze for a moment, then stood up and began pacing. "I'm not understanding. Didn't you just talk to the boys about adopting them?"

"Yes."

"So you've changed your mi—"

"No." Jessie shot to her feet and held up one

hand. The biscuit in her lap hit the porch floor and broke open, scattering across the wood planks. "I'm still going through with the adoption. There's no doubt about that."

Zoe stopped pacing and faced her. "Then, what's going on? I don't understand why you would—"

"Holt showed up here last week. He knocked on the door and asked for my help in reconnecting with Cody and Devin."

"And you agreed?"

"No. Not at first. I absolutely refused." Jessie rubbed her temples where a painful throb had taken up residence. "But then Devin came home from school after getting in trouble over Marjorie Middleton's essay about her dad, and he said he didn't want a dad, but it was right there in the essay he wrote for class, and Holt gave me the card asking me to help him find Cody and Devin on the same day and that just couldn't be a coinciden—"

Zoe sighed. "Jessie, please make this make sense."

"The boys still want a father." Jessie's breath caught, the pain of saying it aloud cutting deeper than she'd expected. "You and I both know that and I... I can't ignore it." Her lower lip trembled. She raked her teeth over it and rolled her shoulders. "I'm going to adopt Cody

and Devin—nothing's going to change that—
but I can't ignore Cody and Devin's needs in
the process. And I've done some checking on
Holt and he seems to have tried to turn his life
around and he's adamant about wanting to be
in the boys' lives, so I thought if I introduced
Holt as a handyman, a stranger, then their meeting would be less risky to the boys. I think this
strategy might be an opportunity for Cody and
Devin to meet Holt in a way that I can still control the situation and protect them. If I don't
agree to some sort of compromise, Holt may
pursue legal action and that'd be the worst thing
for the boys." She waved her hands helplessly
in the air. "I can't explain it, but I feel like I'm
being called to do this. For whatever reason."

Zoe watched her wordlessly.

"Is it a mistake?" Jessie asked. "Please tell
me if I'm doing the wrong thing."

Zoe shook her head, a humorless smile
briefly appearing. "You know I have no way of
knowing that." She reached out and squeezed
Jessie's hand. "But if you feel this is something you need to do—if you think it's best
for Cody and Devin—then you know you have
my support."

Jessie nodded. "I need to do this. The way I
see it, Cody and Devin will have a chance to
meet and have a man in their lives for a little

while, and Holt will see the amount of work, dedication and responsibility that's involved in caring for two children. By the end of his stay, he'll be satisfied with having met them and will realize they're better off with me and then he'll be on his way."

"And if the opposite happens?" Concern clouded Zoe's eyes. "If Holt decides he wants to be their father on a permanent basis? That he wants to take them away from you?"

Jessie recalled the awkward set of his arms as he'd held Ava. The sheer look of terror on his face as she'd cried. "He won't. The way I see it, this is a passing urge on Holt's part prompted by guilt. Giving him a close-up view of the work involved in raising two boys will nip that in the bud. And by not knowing who he really is, the boys will be no worse for wear when he walks away this time. Then the boys and I can start our lives together."

"Like I said, I'll support you," Zoe said. "But I have a bad feeling about this."

"That's why I want you to meet him. You're great at sizing people up—always have been. Just meet him, listen to him, and if he comes across as too shady to be allowed on the property, tell me and this is over."

Zoe smirked. "And if I think he's okay to stick around?"

Jessie shrugged. "Shake his hand or something. Just give me a sign you're comfortable with him staying in the Creek Cabin on a temporary basis and meeting the boys."

"You plan on puttin' him in the Creek Cabin?" Zoe scoffed. "Why ask for my opinion? Just show him where he'll be staying and if he doesn't hightail it out of here right then, you'll know he's in it for the long haul."

A low rumble sounded in the distance and moments later, a large truck rounded the curve and turned in to the driveway, moving slowly toward the cabin.

"Please," Jessie prompted urgently. "Please help me out."

Zoe glanced at the truck that rolled to a stop several feet from the porch. "All right," she murmured. "I still feel like someone's gonna get their heart broken. Let's just hope it's not the boys."

The driver's-side door of the truck opened, and Holt slid out, unfolding his muscular stature to its full six-foot-plus height.

"That's him?" Zoe stared as he strode across the lawn, his long strides eating up the distance between them. She glanced at Jessie then back at Holt and an expression of dismay appeared as she released a low whistle. "Mercy."

Chapter Six

For years, Holt had ambled up to bullpens, straddled thousand-pound beasts and firmed his grip for a back-breaking ride without so much as a sweat. But approaching two stern-faced females sizing him up from above… well, that inspired terror the likes of which he'd never known.

"I, uh…" He halted at the bottom step of Jessie's cabin and eyed Jessie and a blonde woman he didn't recognize who stood by her side. Eyes narrowed and fists propped on their hips, they returned his stare. "I assume it's safe for me to join you?"

The blonde's lips twitched.

"Yes." Jessie broke rank first, gesturing toward a rustic rocking chair that faced her and the blonde on the porch. "Please have a seat. I have something I'd like to discuss with you."

He hesitated, glancing at the blonde's solemn expression once more, then climbed the porch steps and sat in the rocking chair Jessie had indicated.

After a few uncomfortable moments of silence, he drummed his fingertips on the armrests of his chair. "So…you called, I came. What's this about?"

Jessie rubbed her hands together briskly. "I have a proposition for you. A compromise of sorts that I hope you'll consider. The boys are in school right now, so it's a good time to talk."

She was nervous. Despite the firm set of her features, the soft curves of her mouth trembled, and her knuckles whitened as she clenched her hands together in front of her. In spite of it all, his tense muscles sagged with an odd mix of sympathy and relief. Her thick shell of composure had cracked just a bit, and that brief glimpse of vulnerability provoked a protective instinct he hadn't expected.

He eased back in the chair and nodded encouragingly. "Please go on. I was happy you called. As I've told you, I'm eager to see Cody and Devin so I'm willing to hear you out."

"Meet Cody and Devin." The trembling stopped and her mouth thinned into a tight line.

He frowned. "What?"

"You're eager to *meet* Cody and Devin," she repeated. "Not see them. They're no longer the infants you knew. They're seven-year-old boys with unique personalities, strengths and weaknesses, likes and dislikes, fears and—"

"Yeah." He leaned forward, propped his elbows on his knees and met her gaze head-on. "I get it. Again, that's why I'm here."

The blonde cleared her throat and scooted closer to Jessie's side. "Seems like a good time to introduce myself since no one else is going to." She leaned back against the porch rail, her blue eyes surveying him. "I'm Zoe Price, Jessie's friend and assistant manager. I help run Hummingbird Haven, take care of the kids, maintain the grounds and whatnot."

"Thanks for having me." He stood and held out his hand. "I'm Holt Williams, Cody and Devin's father. Though I'm guessing you already know that."

Zoe stared, unblinking, at him and made no move to accept his hand.

Holt sat back down. A rueful grin rose to his lips. "Not the friendliest of welcomes, but that's neither here nor there." He looked at Jessie. "Since you've been up-front with me, I feel it's only fair that I be honest with you. I've agreed to your requests so far with very few—if any—complaints." That slight tremble returned to her mouth. Ignoring it, he quelled the urge to soften his tone and continued, "But I have my limits, too, Jessie. I'm not invulnerable to insult and though I'll admit I've made mistakes—more mistakes than any one man should make in life—I'm also not willing to pay for them indefinitely."

The confident light in her eyes dimmed.

"Tell me what you have planned and I'll consider it," he said. "But please leave out the insulting recriminations, and keep in mind that cooperating with you is not the only option I have to *meeting* my sons."

Her mouth parted and her lashes fluttered rapidly, hiding her eyes as she looked at his boots.

Man, this was not how he'd expected this morning to go. Her invitation for him to visit, bag in hand, had excited him into hoping for the prospect of seeing his sons or, at the very least, having an opportunity to be close to them here at Hummingbird Haven for more than a brief encounter.

But his sons weren't even here at the moment and already, he'd allowed his pride to goad him into sparring with her.

"Look, I'm not trying to be hard here," he said softly. "And I know you have valid doubts about me. I'm just trying to get you to compromise with me respectfully to some degree. Even with what little experience I've had with Cody and Devin, I know it's better for my—" her head shot up, her angry expression halting him midsentence "—*our*...okay? As a figure of speech, it's better for our sons if we go about this with some civility between us."

She considered this and he eased back in his chair again, rocking slowly to the distant chirps of birds and snaps of twigs under burrowing squirrels' feet.

A spring breeze whistled below the cabin's roof, swept across the porch and tugged an errant strand of bright hair across Jessie's freckled cheek. She swept it back absently then sighed and faced him again.

"Okay. I agree." She braced her hands behind her on the porch rail, similar to Zoe's pose, and dipped her head. "Civility. That'll be my goal for the duration of what I'm about to propose."

He stopped rocking. "And how long will that be?"

"For as long as either you—or I—decide is best suited for Cody and Devin." She crossed her feet at the ankles, her well-worn jeans clinging to her shapely legs. He pulled his gaze away and focused on her face as she continued, "What I'm suggesting is that you take up temporary residence here at Hummingbird Haven."

He sat up, the rocking chair dipping beneath his weight as he scooted forward.

She held up a hand. "Temporarily. And on a possibly unwelcome condition."

"Very unwelcome," Zoe murmured.

Jessie shot her a sidelong glance then returned her attention to him. "We have a few cabins on the property that need renovations or updating but we're strapped for cash at the moment, so Zoe's been unable to find anyone willing to do the work for what we'd be able to pay them. My thinking is, you want time with Cody and Devin, and we need a strong hand around the place, so it'd be a nice trade-off if you worked for us during the day and had some time to spend with the boys in the afternoons after school." She bit her lip. "We can't afford to pay you anything other than what we would've offered someone we hired, but I figure instead of money, we'd offer you room and board. Free meals, time with the boys." She motioned toward the surrounding woods and mountain range in the distance. "Whatever equipment you'd need to take advantage of what the mountains have to offer."

"There're great fishing holes all over," Zoe said, crossing her feet, too. "Lots of trails, if you like to hike. And now that it's spring, there'll be plenty of warmer nights for camping, if that's your thing. We have bonfires and s'mores with the kids on the weekends sometimes."

"It won't all be fun and games," Jessie said. "You'll be expected to work, and when I say work, I mean manual labor. Zoe and I have repaired everything our collective muscle can move so the biggest projects on the property are what's left and that's where you'd come in."

Holt nodded. "Of course. I'm used to hard work, and utilizing muscle was my career for several years."

"What about your family's farm?" Jessie asked. "Won't they need you?"

"Yeah, but I'm due for some time off and my family's very understanding when it comes to Cody and Devin."

Her brows rose and he could almost see the gears grinding in her mind. Her unspoken question: *If they were so understanding, where were they seven years ago?*

"I was estranged from my mother and brother for years, but ever since I returned home and they found out about Cody and Devin, they've been nothing but supportive." He smiled at the thought of Liam and his mom seeing Cody and Devin for the first time, knowing he'd reunited with them. "They'll be ecstatic when they hear I'm with them, and they'll be champing at the bit to meet them, too."

A soft sound emerged from Zoe's direction. She shifted from one foot to the other as Jessie pushed off the porch rail and straightened.

"That's the thing," Jessie said. "I don't think it's a good idea for you or your family to jump right in with Cody and Devin. I think it'd do more harm than good to the boys and you if they know who you are."

Holt tensed. "What do you mean if they know who I am? How else would they—"

"We won't tell them you're their father," Jessie said. "We'll tell them you're Hummingbird Haven's new temporary live-in handyman. That's all they'll need to know."

Holt's breathing quickened. His gaze flicked from Jessie to Zoe. "For now?"

Zoe looked down. Rubbed the heel of one of her tennis shoes over the toe of the other.

"For possibly forever," Jessie said, lifting her chin at him. "That depends on you."

"How so?"

"Whether, after you've spent some time caring for Cody and Devin, you decide that you're ready to fully commit to co-parenting them."

He sat still, allowing her words to sink in,

then stood, stalked to the opposite end of the porch and braced his hands on the rail, bowing his head. "You're suggesting that I be introduced as a stranger? Some random man off the street?"

The word *stranger* caught in his throat, and he glanced up beneath his lashes, staring at the tops of the cypress trees against the blue sky.

"I think that's the best approach." Jessie's quiet words barely drifted to him on the breeze. "Until we're able to decide a more permanent way to proceed. That way, if you change your mind or the boys don't seem receptive to more than a casual acquaintance, then it won't be as difficult for you to disentangle yourself and move on with little consequence or pain to Cody and Devin. Or...yourself."

"A stranger," he repeated, his throat constricting. A man of no importance or significance. An untrustworthy nomad of no consequence. His mouth twisted. "It's nothing I haven't been before." Exhaling heavily, he raised his head toward the sky and closed his eyes. "I don't prefer it, but you know Cody and Devin the best and I want a chance to get to know my boys. If you say it's the right thing to do, I'm willing to give it a try."

It was quiet for a while then footsteps shuffled across the porch and Zoe's voice emerged at his back. "Welcome to Hummingbird Haven, Holt."

Slowly, he turned, eyed Zoe's outstretched hand then shook it.

This was either the smartest or dumbest idea of Jessie's life, and she was afraid she wouldn't know which until it was too late.

"Creek Cabin is where we're putting you," she said, glancing over her shoulder.

Holt, treading a couple feet behind her on the dirt trail, hitched his bulky overnight bag over his shoulder and glanced at the thick line of trees on both sides of them. "How many acres do y'all have here?"

"Twenty-six." She kicked a rock off the trail. "We have eight cabins—six of which Zoe and I have already renovated and one of which serves as Hummingbird Haven's community cabin. All our cabins are surrounded by relatively untouched hardwood forest and have great views of the Blue Ridge Mountain range."

"Must've cost a pretty penny to secure this lot."

Jessie harrumphed. "You have no idea." The dirt trail forked off into three gravel trails, all leading in different directions. She veered left and motioned for him to follow. "We caught a break, though. The previous owner used to run this place as a summer camp for local kids but over the years, interest waned. According to her, it was hard to promote an internet-free retreat to kids who were born digital natives. So the property sat empty for over a decade. She was in her fifties when she lost her husband, who helped her keep up the place, and she had no desire to undertake a complete overhaul of the property. She decided to unload it for a reduced price, pocket the cash and relocate closer to her daughter and grandchildren in Florida. And when she learned of my plans to create a shelter, she reduced the price even more, helped us secure funding from a few local businesses that used to fund her and her husband's camp and made a hefty donation herself."

"How long had she and her husband lived here?"

"Oh, around thirty years, I think."

"It's beautiful land. Must've been hard for her to let it go."

"It was." Jessie shrugged. "But she believed in our cause and is much happier being closer to her family. She sends us a Christmas card with a donation every year."

They continued walking in silence for a while, following the winding gravel trail past thick underbrush, ducking beneath low-hanging branches along the way. Finally, they reached a small clearing littered with fallen leaves, wild vines and uneven slopes. A log cabin with a wide porch slumped on the back of the lot in front of thick woods and a deep, rocky creek whose bubbling waters filled their surroundings with a rhythmic rush.

"It's not much to look at." Jessie glanced at Holt. His guarded expression revealed very little. "But I promise you it's sound." Her step slowed as they ascended onto the front porch. "Except for the back deck that borders the creek. Several of the wood planks have rotted and I'm afraid it's not safe to venture out on it until they've been replaced."

One corner of his mouth lifted. "I suppose that's one of the instances where I come in?"

She smiled. "Yeah."

He renewed his grip on the bag slung over his shoulder and spun slowly around, surveying the property. Her eyes followed his gaze, taking in the patches of overgrown grass, scattered wildflowers and jagged rocks, as well as a fallen tree and nearby fire pit surrounded by three log benches, each one covered with twisting vines.

What were those pesky vines anyway? She scratched her arm. Poison ivy, maybe?

"The yard's gonna need some attention." He leaned to the side and craned his neck, taking in the trees towering over the cabin. "And I see another tree or two that're probably gonna hit the ground—or cabin—the next time a stiff breeze pushes through."

"Yep. That's on your to-do list, too."

He looked at her, a rueful expression crossing his handsome face. "Any chance I can get a copy of that to-do list?"

"Soon." Dodging his gaze, she opened the front door and motioned for him to follow. "For now, I'll show you the digs and let you get your bearings."

Musty air hit her as soon as she stepped inside, clogging her throat and wrinkling her nose. Stifling a cough, she hustled over to the small window by the door and tugged. "I should've thought to open this up a couple weeks ago when it started getting warmer."

It didn't budge.

She leaned into it and yanked harder, wincing as it creaked but didn't open. "Uh, it works, I promise. It just—" she yanked again "—needs a bit of—" another yank "—elbow gr—"

Two big hands covered hers, blunt thumbs tucking under the bottom of the window, then pulled, opening the window with a *swoosh*.

"Oof!" Jessie stumbled forward and yanked

Holt, who still held a firm grip on the window, with her, tumbling his brawny frame into the back of hers and smooshing her cheek against the rusty screen.

He recovered first, pushing himself upright and tugging her with him by her shoulders. "Sorry about that." His forefinger gently flicked a speck of rust from her cheek. "Just wanted to help."

Face heating, she stepped away and blew a strand of hair out of her eyes. "Yeah, well..."

She clasped her hands together, trying not to notice the way his strong, callused touch still lingered on her skin. It wasn't him, per se, she reassured herself. It was the sensation of support that stirred her attention; that was all. The security of a firm, steady presence she was unaccustomed to having around.

"I appreciate your help," she forced out gruffly. "I mean, that's one of the major benefits of having you stay here."

His brow creased. "Besides spending time with Cody and Devin, you mean?"

She rubbed her left shoulder, right where his wide palm had settled briefly. "Yes, of course."

"Because I'm trusting you, Jessie."

She stilled as the directness of his hazel eyes locked on to hers.

"Just as much as you're trusting me," he

added. "Or trying to trust me." A muscle in his sculpted jaw ticked. "If you're angling for a leg up in any part of this situation, you should know it's not easy to take advantage of me... even if I am desperate to be a part of Cody and Devin's lives."

"I know." She lifted her chin. "And you should know I'm not easy to take advantage of, either."

His tone softened as he grinned. "No. Of that, I'm certain."

Maybe it was the gentle way he said the words, or it might've been that tempting grin he sported, but either way, she relaxed, her own smile rising easily to her lips.

"Good. Because I'd hate for you to find out the hard way." She eased past him and led the way through to the kitchen. "As you can probably tell by now, this is one of our smallest cabins. There's an electric stove, a fridge and a microwave that works great." She waited as he looked around then led him down the narrow hallway. "There's one bathroom—" she opened a door to the right "—shower, toilet, sink. And the one bedroom is over here."

She opened the door on the left and gestured toward the double bed with a bare mattress and a single dresser without a mirror.

He grimaced. "You trying to run me off already?"

She leaned against the doorjamb as he walked over to the bed, dumped his bag on the mattress. "No, not at all. But the rest of our cabins are either in use, reserved to shelter new residents who will arrive soon or in the process of final renovations, so this is the best of what's available."

He crossed the room and opened the sole window in the bedroom, breathing deep as fresh air billowed in. "It'll do. Thank you."

"You're welcome. I haven't stocked supplies here yet and I wasn't exactly sure what you might need, so you'll need to run into town tonight and pick up groceries and toiletries. I'll give you money for that, of course. It's part of the room and board we'll provide."

He faced her, propped his hands on his lean hips and cocked one blond eyebrow. "You agree that we're going to work together as a true team? Honesty and trust on both sides?"

What was it his friend Ty had said? *Old habits die hard.*

It'd be easy to come clean. Tell Holt right now, this second, that she still didn't trust him. That she may never trust him. But…she had to start somewhere, for Cody and Devin's sakes.

She nodded. "Yes. I agree."

Holt smiled, flashing his perfect white teeth and mischievous charm. Two of his many attractive attributes that made a normally sensible woman, such as herself, doubt her ability to trust the tempting scoundrel. "I assume it'll be a while before the boys get home?" At her nod, he asked, "So what now?"

Jessie gritted her teeth, dragged her attention away from his handsome face and left the room. "We work."

Chapter Seven

Of all the potential tasks with which Holt imagined Jessie might entrust him, one involving an ax had never crossed his mind.

"You sure you trust me with this?" Standing outside Creek Cabin with said ax in hand, Holt cocked one eyebrow and eyed Jessie over a large pile of logs. "I mean, there're no limit to the amount of malicious damage a ne'er-do-well stranger—" he touched one hand to his chest "—such as myself, might do with one of these."

Jessie hefted a thick log from the pile, tossed it toward two sturdy chopping stumps nearby, then picked up a second ax that lay on the grass by the log pile and grinned. A bit sarcastically, he had to admit. "Not if I have one, too." Her tone turned teasing as she slapped the handle of the ax with her free hand. "I'm pretty adept at chopping and there's no telling which of your appendages I'd remove first. Just try something amiss and see what happens."

Ah, so there was a bit of humor hiding behind that stern expression of hers. He'd wondered after her abrupt departure earlier in the cabin whether she truly agreed with him in terms of working as a trusting team. The soft tone of her voice had changed at his mention of it, turning harder and possibly…angry.

Of course, he'd expected that. When he'd received her call yesterday asking him to pack a bag and return to Hummingbird Haven, he had prepared himself to bear the brunt of all sorts of emotions from her and possibly Cody and Devin—if she'd been willing to let him near them. So when she stalked out of the cabin before, he had unpacked his clothes from his bag and given her some breathing room.

The technique had paid off. She'd returned about a half hour later, calmer and seemingly more welcoming, and asked him to follow her outside for the first task of the day. Who knew what he was in for during his days of working with her, and a laugh or two mixed into their time together was a welcome relief.

He smiled. "Don't think I'll chance it, thank you. I think I've been around you enough now to guess what punishment I'd suffer." Glancing at the massive pile of wood in front of him, he bent, grabbed a log and tossed it next to the one Jessie had thrown. "How much of this wood are we chopping?"

"All of it." She pointed at another massive pile of logs near the edge of the clearing surrounding Creek Cabin. "And that, too. And possibly, if there's time before the boys get home, we'll start hacking up the two trees that fell near the trail as well. Given the number of cabins we have and the guests we expect to continue housing through the winter, we'll need as much firewood as we can round up between now and the end of summer. The earlier it gets chopped and stacked, the better, though. That way it'll have more time to season up properly." She reached into her back pocket and tugged out two pairs of gloves. "Here. You'll need these. Not sure they'll fit, but they're the biggest we have on hand."

Holt caught the gloves she tossed against his chest, unfolded them and tugged one on. "A bit tight, but they'll do." He put on the other glove, flexed his hands and strolled over to one of the chopping stumps. "How long until the boys get home?"

She picked up another heavy log and tossed it on the ground in front of his feet. "'Bout four hours. Zoe picks all the kids up around three and they have snack time right after in our community cabin. I figure we should be able to make it through this pile by two o'clock then we'll go to my cabin, fix the snacks and be ready to meet them when they arrive."

His heart thumped against his ribs with an onslaught of emotions—excitement, fear, nervous tension and anxiety—at the thought of seeing Cody and Devin. Focusing on the task, he grabbed a log, balanced it on a chopping stump and gripped the ax handle with both hands. "Do they like school?"

"Yeah." She tossed another log on the ground beside the chopping stumps. "Especially recess."

He chuckled, swung the ax and split the log with one strike. "That sounds about right."

"About right for what?" Joining him, Jessie placed a log on the chopping stump nearest her and glanced at the two halves of the log resting on his stump.

"About right for how Liam and I were about that age." He tossed the split halves of the log onto a patch of dirt to his left. "Liam was always more studious—more serious—than I was, but even he could put worry in Ms. Whitham's eyes when he was cut loose in the wilds of the playground for recess."

"Ms. Whitham?"

He balanced another log on the stump. "Our first-grade teacher." Laughing, he split the log in half with one swing. "She always had to keep an extra eye on us. And the good Lord help her if one of us got ahold of a jump rope."

Jessie braced her legs apart and swung, cutting about a third of the way into her log. She frowned, eyed his second split log, then swung again. It cracked another third of the way down. "What'd you two do with a jump rope?"

He tossed the split logs on the dirt, grabbed another and split it. "We liked to tie each other to the jungle gym, upside down." Chuckling, he split another log. "Sometimes, we used the seesaw. Liam liked me to lie on my back on one end, he'd tie me down, then jump on the other end and give me the ride of my life." He tossed the halves onto the dirt. "What about Cody and Devin? They ever get into mischief?"

She swung her ax, finally splitting her log. "They're not quite that rambunctious, but they certainly have their days."

He paused as she grabbed another log, eyed his stump again then swung. The ax only made it halfway through the log. "And you? Were you mischievous when you were a kid?"

She glanced at him, surprise flickering

through her expression, then returned her attention to the log in front of her. "Not really."

Hmm. That was hard to imagine, Holt thought. As headstrong and determined as she was, he'd imagined she would've been a handful at that age. "Not even a bit? You mean, you never got into trouble as a kid?"

She swung her ax again, gaining another inch into the log. "No." The ax was stuck. She propped her heel on the log and yanked with both arms, prying the ax head free. "Why? What would you expect me to have been like?"

He rubbed his jaw. Studied her long auburn ponytail flopping over her shoulder with the next swing of her ax. Eyed the cute freckles scattered across the bridge of her nose. He grinned. "I don't know. Tidy pigtails, strong right hook and an attitude."

Cheeks reddening, she batted a fly away from her glistening face and swung again. Finally, the log split in half. She grabbed another.

"What about as a teen?" he asked. "You find trouble then?"

Her mouth tightened. Eyes glued to the log on the stump, she swung the ax again. Still, she didn't answer.

"Did you grow up 'round here?" he prompted. "Your parents live nearby?"

Another swing, this time missing the log and striking the stump instead.

His grin fell. He watched as she rebalanced the log on the stump, braced her legs apart and swung again. "This isn't a competition, you know."

"Oh, I know." She dropped the ax to her side, leaning on it as the blade dug into the dirt. "I'm working on these logs while you're just jawing."

Her tone bit. The mean cut of it was so out of touch with the mission she'd dedicated herself to here at Hummingbird Haven and the compassionate way she'd greeted him that night seven years ago.

Holt studied her tight expression, and she returned his scrutiny, those dark brown eyes of hers piercing into his. But this time they were clouded with something else. Some deep-seated pain.

Yeah. There was something there. Something she hid mighty deep, if his suspicions were correct.

"I didn't mean the firewood," he said quietly. "I meant—" he gestured between them "—you and I. We're not supposed to be working against each other. We've agreed to work together. And seeing as how you know quite a bit about me, I don't see the harm in getting to know you better."

He stopped, an unfamiliar sensation unfurling in his chest. A hint of what? Want? Desire? No...*need*. A need so different from any he'd felt in the past for other women. A tender curiosity. One that had nothing to do with physical attraction, though it was impossible to deny he certainly felt that for her, too. But this was something else. Something he'd never felt before. A different kind of curiosity. One he hoped she'd acquire for him, too.

"I'd like very much to get to know you better," he said softly. To get inside her head and see the world as she saw it. Hear her thoughts and fears, wishes and dreams. To get inside her heart and...?

"You know me well enough." She snatched the ax back into the air and braced her legs. "And as your teammate," she stressed, "what I'd appreciate the most in this moment is for you to help me chop this pile of wood."

The ax flew downward under the momentum of her swinging arms, splitting the log on the stump with one strike, the cracking wood echoing against the thick woods surrounding them, abruptly ending the conversation.

Sighing, he grabbed another log, positioned it on the stump in front of him and hefted his ax back into his hands. It was probably best he focus his energy on preparing to meet with Cody and Devin this afternoon. He'd do as she asked and let it go. For now.

Four hours later Holt chopped his twelfth cucumber in Jessie's kitchen, picked up the cutting board and dumped the slices onto a large paper plate. "Surely these kids won't down all these cheese, crackers and cucumbers." His nose wrinkled. "Especially the cucumbers."

Jessie, standing beside him, reached across the kitchen island for a cucumber. Her bare arm brushed his and her soft, fresh scent whispered against his nose. "You got something against cucumbers?"

"No, but they're not my favorite kind of vegetable. If I were a kid, I'd go for the cream cheese first. Or better yet, I'd wish there was some peanut butter and jelly."

"Not as healthy," she said.

He caught himself leaning closer as she placed the cucumber on her cutting board and chopped, her movements releasing another sweetly scented breeze to his senses. Good night above, how had she managed to keep that intoxicating scent through three and a half hours of chopping wood, stacking logs and trekking dirt trails back to her cabin?

He spun away, tossed his knife into the sink and turned on the tap, shoving his wet fingers beneath the running water. A squirt of the moisturizing lavender gel soap on the counter got rid of the cucumbers seeds on his fingers and left his hands feeling clean and rejuvenated.

Man, how he wished he could say the same for the rest of him. Unlike Jessie, three and a half hours of outdoor manual labor had wrung what felt like every drop of sweat from his body, soaked his T-shirt and dampened his jeans, leaving his clothes clinging to him uncomfortably and, he suspected, emitting an unpleasant smell in his wake.

He plucked his sweaty shirt from his chest and fanned it, hoping to dissipate the odor. "I don't suppose I have enough time to run back to my cabin and take a shower?"

The steady chop of Jessie's knife continued. "Nope." Finished, she dumped the cucumber slices into a container then joined him at the sink to wash her hands. "Zoe should be pulling up any minute now with the kids and we still have to transport everything to the community cabin. Plus, I asked Peggy Ann to get permission from her supervisor to end her shift early at the hardware store and come as well."

"Peggy Ann?"

"Yeah. She and her two daughters, Tabitha and Katie, have been living here for a couple months now. I thought it'd be best if you met everyone at once and it's very important that we stick to the usual schedule. That's your first lesson," she said. "Kids—especially kids in Cody and Devin's situation—need structure."

Wonderful. His first encounter with Hummingbird Haven's guests and his sons would be overpowered by his sweat, grime and stink. Not exactly how he'd pictured the reunion.

Wincing, Holt rubbed the back of his neck. "You sure there's no time for a shower? I'd be real quick."

"Relax. I know you're nervous and I was hoping for a little downtime before everyone got here, but it just didn't work out that way."

"But I'm soaked with sweat." He fanned his shirt faster. "And I have a feeling I stink."

Hands clean, she grabbed the dish towel and dried them. "I haven't noticed anything. I mean you might." She leaned close and sniffed, her lips quirking. "Oh, well…maybe you do need a little something." She tossed the dish towel back into the dish drying rack. "How 'bout you run to your cabin and put on a little deodorant? I think that'd do the trick."

"That's the thing." He rubbed the back of his neck. "I ran out of deodorant and body wash yesterday and used up the last bit of the stuff in those little bottles they give you at the motel, so I'm out. Fresh out of everything. I'd planned on stocking back up but then you called and invited me here and now, seeing as how there's nothing in the cabin—"

"Oh." She made a face. "I wasn't certain you'd go for my proposal, so I didn't think far enough ahead."

He waved away her concern. "Not your fault. I should've grabbed something on the way here."

"Hold up." She left the kitchen and headed down a hallway. "Think I can help."

Holt returned to the sink, turned on the faucet and lowered his head, splashing water on his face and neck. Barely a birdbath, at best, but it was the best option for the moment.

"Here you go." Jessie returned, holding out a small blue deodorant container. "Just picked this up the other day in a discounted two-pack, and this is the one I haven't used yet. It's all yours until you make it to the store later this afternoon."

He shut off the faucet, wiped his face with the dish towel then took the deodorant from her and glanced at the label. Pink flowers and white daisies sent a shudder through him. "Wildflower Delight?"

Jessie smiled. A bit too wide for his liking. "Yep."

He stared. "This is for women."

She smiled bigger. "But you know what they say, it's strong enough—"

"Nuh-uh." He held it back out to her. "Nope."

"Come on. You said you needed something, and I provided it. Give and take." She nudged his arm and winked. "Like a team, you know?"

"Seriously?" He narrowed his eyes. "You're enjoying this, aren't you?"

She shrugged. "Use it or don't use it, it's up to you. But there aren't any other men living here, so there's no chance of finding a more manly scent." Returning to the island, she fastened the top on the large container of cucumbers as well as two others on additional containers loaded with crackers and herbed cream cheese. "You need to make up your mind soon, though, because they'll be here any minute and you're in charge of bringing the napkins, cups and sweet tea to the community cabin."

With that, she stacked the sandwich containers in her arms and headed for the door.

Holt stared at the deodorant in his hand and weighed his options. Unfortunately, there weren't many. He uncapped the deodorant, took a deep whiff, then, shaking his head, lifted his shirt and applied it liberally, hoping it'd help him seem slightly more presentable.

The screen door of Jessie's cabin squeaked, and her voice drifted back into the kitchen. "Come on. The van's pulling in the driveway."

Quickly, he shoved the deodorant in his back pocket, grabbed the cardboard box containing packs of napkins, plastic cups and two jugs of sweet tea and walked outside.

Sure enough, a large van was slowly making its way down the winding driveway toward the community cabin Jessie had pointed out to him earlier that afternoon. He hustled alongside the vehicle, falling in step beside Jessie as she waved in the direction of a chorus of voices calling down from the van's open windows.

Hi, Jessie! We're home! and *What're we eating?* quickly gave way to stunned silence at the sight of him. Then one young voice, curious with a hint of suspicion, called out, "Who's he?"

Holt glanced up and sought out the owner of the voice. A blond boy with hazel eyes and familiar features frowned back at him. Moments later a second blond boy with identical features but an excited expression shoved his face into the window's opening to stare down at him as well.

Cody and Devin. His sons.

Holt's hands trembled and his grip slipped on the box he carried. Feeling Jessie's eyes on him, he renewed his grip on the box and refocused on the path ahead.

"Remember," Jessie said below the rumble of the van's engine as it passed. "You're the new live-in handyman. Nothing more."

He glanced at her, unable to stop two firm words from escaping his lips. "For now."

She held his gaze for two steps then picked up the pace, edged in front of him and led the way up the front stairs into the community cabin.

By the time Holt made it inside, set the cardboard box on one of the wide dining tables and unpacked its contents, Zoe opened the front door of the community cabin and ushered the kids inside.

"Come on, my young ones," Zoe called. "I heard through the grapevine that there's a special surprise in store for y'all this afternoon so please be on your best behavior."

A cacophony of kids' voices filled the entryway as they filed in, their eyes eagerly scanning the room and freezing when they encountered Holt. The voices quickly lowered to barely discernable whispers as they each took a seat at a table to the left of him and stared in his direction.

There were five children total: two girls with brown hair, one in her teens and the other looked to be a bit younger, a young boy with black hair and frightened eyes who couldn't be more than five or six and, of course, Cody and Devin.

Holt stilled, his eyes glued to the two boys who sat next to each other, staring up at him with wide, unblinking eyes. Excitement and fear bubbled up from his middle and weakened his legs.

He bit his lip. Imagine that. He'd been thrown across arenas by thousand-pound bulls hard enough to break his back on more than one occasion and he'd rolled over in the dirt, shot to his feet and walked away smiling. But one look from these two boys—*his sons*—and he lost his balance, his heart bursting with love, pride, regret, guilt, fear and anticipation. He'd never felt anything like it before.

"Hi, everyone!" A tall woman with brown hair the same shade as the two girls sitting at the table walked in, waving at the kids. She glanced at Jessie, Zoe then Holt, her next words trailing away. "Hope I'm not late…"

Jessie followed the woman's gaze to Holt and strode to his side quickly, speaking in a calm tone. "Not at all, Peggy Ann. You're right on time." She gestured toward the table where the kids were seated. "Please have a seat and get comfortable. We have an introduction to make and I'm glad everyone could be here at one time." She surveyed the crowded table before her then looked at Holt. A glimmer of uncertainty flickered through her gaze before she blinked, dashing it away. "We have a new guest that'll be staying with us temporarily."

Was it him, or did she add extra emphasis to *temporarily*?

"Holt Wil—er, *Mr. Holt* is what we ask you to refer to him as—has joined us here at Hummingbird Haven and will be serving as our handyman," she continued. "He'll be staying in Creek Cabin and will renovate that cabin as well as Hummingbird Hollow on the outskirts of the property. I hope you'll provide him a warm welcome."

Jessie and Zoe clapped their hands in welcome and nodded encouragingly at the kids. Each child slowly joined in, clapping quietly, their wide eyes still taking him in. The expressions on their faces were similar—tense and suspicious.

Tough crowd. Holt shifted nervously from one foot to the other. Perhaps he should make a concerted effort to greet them properly, too. Make himself friendly and approachable.

Clearing his throat, he walked over to one

end of the table where the woman named Peggy Ann sat, bent and held out his hand. "Nice to meet y—"

The woman, fear flashing through her expression, visibly shrank back in her chair, and the two girls sitting by her side huddled closer, apprehension in their eyes.

Holt withdrew his hand immediately and stepped back. "I—I'm sorry. I didn't mean to—"

"It's okay," Zoe said, walking over to Peggy Ann's side. She reached down and squeezed the other woman's shoulder. "Everyone can take as long as they like getting to know each other, and Holt understands that the space and time needed will be different for everyone. Things will continue exactly as they have before, and you'll all still be in control of your surroundings. Holt will respect your boundaries and leave your immediate area anytime you ask him to." She looked at Holt. "Right?"

Taken aback, he nodded. "Yes." He nodded again. "Of course." He glanced at Cody and Devin, who still eyed him from afar, then looked at Peggy Ann, who still seemed disconcerted by his presence. "If you'd like me to leave while you visit with the kids, I c—"

"No." Voice shaking, Peggy Ann squeezed her hands together in her lap and smiled up at him. It was strained. "I—I'm just a little tired, is all." She looked at Jessie—almost desperately. "We had a busy day at the hardware store today. That's why I'm a bit jumpy."

Jessie smiled gently. "There's no need to explain, Peggy Ann—ever. This is your home. You're entitled to be open with how you feel and what you want. Everyone here will respect that."

"It's a rule," Cody—or maybe it was Devin?—piped from the other end of the table.

"Absolutely." Jessie winked. "Which brings me to the invitation of the day." She looked at Holt. "Holt, would you mind if anyone would like to introduce themselves to you up close?"

His throat was dry. He swallowed hard, eyeing his sons expectantly. "No, not at all."

Jessie spread her arms. "Any takers?"

Silence fell across the room. Peggy Ann looked down, along with the two girls at her side, whom he assumed were her daughters. The youngest boy took an immediate interest in his napkin, folding it intently as though undertaking an artistic work of origami. And Cody and Devin? They continued to stare, unblinking, at him. Neither of them moved and neither of them spoke.

Holt smiled and offered an encouraging look, but it made no difference. Cody and

Devin made no effort to approach him. Maybe Jessie was right. Maybe his sons were happier without a father in their lives than they could ever be with one in it. And the way things were going so far, they might only ever know him as a stranger.

Come on, Lord, he prayed silently, *please let them give me a chance.*

And right then, one of his sons stood up, walked over to Holt's side and said with surprise, "You smell like a girl!"

Chapter Eight

All sorts of scenarios had tumbled around inside Jessie's head when she imagined how a first meeting between Holt and the boys would unfold, but this moment had not been one of them.

Cody, standing beside Holt in Hummingbird Haven's community center, wrinkled his nose and looked back at his brother. "Come see, Devin. He smells just like a girl!"

Devin stood and strolled over to Cody's side. Eyeing Holt, he stuck his chin out in Holt's direction and took a whiff. "Yep." He glanced over his shoulder and frowned at Jessie with disapproval. "He smells like you. And kinda like Marjorie Middleton, too."

Jessie rolled her lips together, stifling a smile. "Boys, commenting on someone's scent is not a very polite way to greet someone."

Though she had to admit, it did tickle her funny bone for some reason.

Aw, who was she kidding? She knew exactly why. Seeing Holt—an imposing masculine tower of sinewy strength—cringe at two boys comparing his scent to that of their six-year-old female arch nemesis was just the moment she needed to set her biggest fears at ease. No way would her boys run out of her arms and blindly into those of a strange man who smelled like Marjorie Middleton.

Frowning, in a remarkably identical way as Devin, Holt looked at her, too. "Who's Marjorie Middleton?"

"Oh, just a girl from school," Zoe said, rounding the table and joining the trio. "And, boys, Mr. Holt does not smell like…" She tilted her head. Sniffed the air a time or two, a perplexed expression appearing on her face as she glanced at Jessie. "Well, he doesn't smell like Marjorie, but he does smell kinda like—"

"Wildflower Delight," Holt grumbled.

Jessie choked back a laugh. "Never mind how he smells, guys." Conscious they had an audience of young, impressionable minds, she continued, "How should you greet someone you first meet, boys?"

Cody faced Holt again, tipped his head back and stuck out his hand. "Nice to meet you,

Mr. Holt. I'm Cody Williams. And this—" he pointed at Devin "—is my brother, Devin."

"Pleased to make your acquaintance," Holt said, his words trembling slightly.

The husky note in his voice and the tenderness in his smile and gaze as he looked down at Cody melted away more than just Jessie's easy smile. Her heart warmed unexpectantly at Holt's reverent approach to his sons.

Holt shook Cody's hand, his own brawny palm enveloping the little boy's small one, then he released Cody's hand somewhat reluctantly, it seemed, and held his upturned palm out to his other son. "Devin. It's an honor."

More difficult to impress than his brother, Devin walked past Holt's outstretched arm and circled his brawny frame, eyeing him from head to toe. "When'd you get here?"

Holt straightened and smiled down at Devin. "This morning." He motioned toward his sweat-stained shirt. "Started working first thing."

"What'd you work on?" Cody asked, trailing in Devin's footsteps as he continued circling Holt.

"Firewood." A slow smile lifted Holt's lips as he watched his sons stroll slowly around him with prying eyes. "I helped Jessie chop up a pile out by Creek Cabin."

."That's where you're staying tonight, right?" Devin asked.

Holt nodded.

"And tomorrow, and the next?" Cody asked.

"Yep."

Devin stared at Holt's feet. "Your boots are old."

Holt's slow grin widened. "'Cuz I use them a lot. They're broken in just right. Served me well for a lot of years."

"For doing what?" Devin glanced up, narrowed his eyes. "Repair stuff?"

Holt hesitated. "Among other things."

"What things?" Cody asked.

Holt's gaze met Jessie's and she blinked in surprise at the unspoken question in his eyes. *How much should he share? What was permitted?* Good grief, if only she knew. But the simple fact that he'd looked to her before answering was reassuringly welcome…and strangely disconcerting all at once.

She glanced at the boys then looked back at Holt and nodded.

"I've had other jobs," Holt said quietly.

"Like what?" Cody asked.

Holt's smile returned. "I used to be a professional athlete."

Cody's eyes widened as he surveyed him closer. "What kind?"

"Rodeo."

Devin cocked his head, the first hint of genuine interest sparking in his expression. "Like a cowboy?"

Holt nodded. "I rode bulls, broncs, wrestled steers a few—"

"Bulls?" Devin perked up. "Real bulls? Horns, hooves, snot and all?"

Holt laughed. "Yep. All o' that and then some."

"He's got the muscles for it," Cody told Devin, tugging at Holt's left biceps.

Jessie stepped forward. "Cody, don't do th—"

"It's okay." Holt held up his free hand, stilling her movements, then showed Cody and Devin his palm. "See that? That long, rough patch of skin? That's a callus from holding on."

A breathy sound of awe left Cody's lips. He grabbed Holt's wrist, tugged his palm closer and waved at the other kids still seated at the table. "Come look, Miles! He's a real honest-to-goodness bull rider."

Miles craned his neck for a better view but remained seated at the table with Peggy Ann and her girls.

"Just 'cuz he's got a callus doesn't mean he's a bull rider," Devin scoffed. "Besides, bull riders don't smell like girls."

Holt pursed his lips. "Actually, they do. Some

bull riders are girls, and some of those girls ride better than the boys."

Devin scowled. "Nuh-uh."

"Yeah-huh." Grinning, Holt winked. "You can put your money where your mouth is, but I wouldn't recommend it. Those ladies are tough."

Devin considered this, his scowl easing. "How good were you?"

Holt grinned wider. "I held my own."

"You ever win anything?" Cody asked.

"I've won a few times."

"How many?"

"You get any trophies?"

"Break an arm?"

"Wear a cast?"

Questions continued tumbling out of the boys' mouths, blending together and drowning out Holt's responses.

Jessie stepped in. "That's enough, you two. The snacks are ready and there are others waiting to eat." She gestured toward Miles, Peggy Ann and her daughters, who sat at the table laden with herbed cream cheese, crackers and cucumbers, their gazes darting back and forth between Holt and the boys. "Ms. Peggy Ann took time off her new job to join us, so I say we all have a seat, say the blessing and dig in."

The slew of questions stopped and the boys,

grumbling, complied with her request and took their seats at the table.

Cody patted the chair next to him. "Sit here, Mr. Holt."

Jessie wove her fingers together and squeezed, watching nervously as Holt pulled out the chair Cody had referenced and prepared to sit.

He hesitated and glanced at Peggy Ann, who sat at the other end of the table. "Is this okay with you, Ms. Peggy Ann?"

Peggy Ann surveyed him once more then sat up straighter and nodded stiffly. "Of course."

It was progress. Jessie pressed her sweaty palms together and bit her lip. When Peggy Ann had arrived at Hummingbird Haven—for the third time—two months ago, bruised and bloodied, with her daughters in tow, she'd barely lifted her head to ask Jessie if she could stay. *Just once more*, she'd said, *this time for good, I promise*.

It'd taken several weeks for the bruises to fade and another month for Peggy Ann to summon the courage to lift her head and look Jessie and Zoe in the eye. Since she'd started working at the hardware store—the only job opening at the time of Peggy Ann's job search—and working with the therapist Jessie had provided for her and her daughters, she didn't startle as easily and the low light Jessie had glimpsed in the kitchen window of Peggy Ann's cabin had stopped flickering on at odd hours of the night, Peggy Ann seemingly able to sleep through the night again.

"Thank you," Holt said, sitting beside Cody.

Zoe rubbed her hands together and smiled. "Let's say the blessing."

Fifteen minutes later the containers were empty, and a lone cracker remained amidst scattered crumbs on a serving plate, but there continued to be a never-ending supply of questions from the boys.

"Why do you do this with your arm when you ride?" Cody asked, stretching his left arm above his head and undulating it slowly. A bit of cream cheese fell from his bottom lip onto the table. "Don't it get tired?"

"Cody," Jessie said, "please don't talk when your mouth is full."

"Sorry." He chewed then swallowed. "So don't it, Mr. Holt? Get tired, I mean."

Holt wiped his mouth with his napkin then tossed the napkin onto his empty plate. "Not particularly. Other things get tired a lot faster, and to answer your question, we use that arm to help maintain our balance. Plus, we're not allowed to touch the bull with our free hand."

"But what about when the bull kicks?" Devin asked, popping his last bite of cream cheese and cracker into his mouth. "Doesn't it throw you forward? What do you do when you're about to fall onto the bull's head? And what about the horns? Won't they stab you?"

"Okay, that's it." Jessie folded her unused napkin and placed it neatly on top of her untouched cream cheese and crackers. "That's enough discussion about bull riding. Y'all are wearing Mr. Holt out."

Cody made a face. "But, Jessie—"

"No buts." Jessie stood, grabbed her plate, walked to the end of the table and grabbed a roll of aluminum foil from the box Holt had carried earlier. "I'm sure Mr. Holt is tired of being interrogated." She ripped off a portion of foil, folded it over her plate and glanced at Peggy Ann under her lashes. "Are you feeling okay, Peggy Ann?"

Peggy Ann, her food barely touched, pushed her chair away from the table. "I'm sorry, Jessie. I'm not very hungry this afternoon." She tried—but failed—to smile, her lips barely lifting before they fell again. "If you don't mind, I'd like to take my girls to our cabin and help them with their homework there."

Jessie dipped her head. "Of course. But let me wrap your plate first. You might get hungry later and that snack will come in handy."

After covering Peggy Ann's uneaten food

with foil, Jessie walked with her and the girls to the door and waved goodbye as they walked down the front steps and strolled down the trail toward their cabin.

"…can we go, Jessie?"

A small hand tugged at the hem of her shirt, and she looked down, finding Cody by her side.

"Can I?" he repeated.

Jessie frowned. "Go where?"

"To the store with Mr. Holt later on." Cody, practically bouncing with excitement, glanced over his shoulder at Holt. "He said he has to go get supplies and stuff."

Jessie watched as Holt gathered up the dirty paper plates from the table with Zoe and tossed them into a nearby trash can. Miles disposed of his own dirty plate, cautiously following Holt to the trash can.

"No," she said. "That's not a good idea."

"Why not?" A plaintive tone entered Cody's voice. "We don't got no homework tonight and it ain't even dark yet."

"You don't *have any* homework," Jessie corrected, "and it *isn't* dark yet. And the answer's no."

"But he says he's got to get—" Cody stopped, his brow wrinkling, then continued. "He says he has to get some de-oh…de-oh-du…"

"Deodorant." Devin, walking over, stood on the other side of Jessie and smirked. "He said it's your deodorant that's making him smell like a girl and that he needs to get his own." He looked up at Jessie. "And Cody doesn't need to go anyway."

"Aw, hush it," Cody said. "You don't tell me what I can and can't do."

Devin frowned. "I can tell you whatever I feel li—"

"Okay, okay, that's enough, boys." Jessie rubbed her forehead. "Look, I get that you're excited to meet Mr. Holt, Cody, but today's his first day here and I'm sure he'd rather do his shopping by himself."

"I wouldn't mind." Holt, repacking leftover cups and paper plates into the box on the table, tapped the sides of the cardboard box and shrugged. "I'm just gonna swing by the grocery store and pick up some supplies, is all."

Jessie plucked Cody's fingers off her shirt hem. "Excuse me, boys." She walked over to Holt's side, leaned in and whispered, "Are you serious right now? You just got here. It's not a good idea for you to haul one of the boys off somewhere by yourself."

One blond brow lifted. "Why not?" he whispered back. "You afraid I'll run off with him? I'd never do that to you—or the boys. Besides, it takes what? Eight to ten minutes to get to the store and I'll only be in there for five to ten minutes. That's no more than half an hour to get there and back. You'd barely even notice."

"Oh, I'd notice. I'd notice every second Cody wasn't with me."

Holt sighed. "I didn't mean it like that. You know I didn't." He leaned closer. "But Cody's interested in me. Even you have to admit that. And isn't that the point of me being here? The reason why you invited me? To get to know the boys and for them to become acquainted with me?"

"Yes, but—"

Someone cleared their throat. Zoe poked her head in between Jessie's and Holt's. "You've got three little sets of eyes and ears intently focused on you right now, in case neither of you has noticed," she said softly.

Jessie and Holt straightened slowly and looked around. Sure enough, Cody, Devin and Miles all stood in a neat line on the opposite side of the table, each of them straining forward, their wide eyes fixed on Jessie and Holt and their heads tilted in their direction.

Jessie cleared her throat and Holt shoved his hands into his pockets.

"Look," Zoe whispered, turning her face away from the boys and smoothing her hand over her ponytail. "Maybe it's not such a bad idea." She glanced at Jessie, a small smile appearing as she said sheepishly, "After all, the purpose of you inviting Holt here is—like he said—to get to know the boys. It's a quick trip and making a big deal out of it will only make the boys think you don't trust him, which will make the boys not trust him, either."

Jessie's eyes widened. "Zoe…"

She couldn't believe this. Absolutely could not believe that Zoe would take Holt's side over hers. Especially now—on day one!

"But you…" Jessie's throat ran dry. "You're…"

Right. As always. As much as she hated to admit it, Zoe was absolutely right. A quick trip to the store wasn't a big deal. And she should be happy that Cody, at least, had taken an interest in Holt. But something about this just didn't sit right with her. Too much was happening way too fast right off the bat—disruption to their routine and Cody's immediate admiration for Holt. And what did that mean for the future she'd so carefully planned for herself and the boys? A future in which Holt hadn't figured at all?

"Okay," Jessie mumbled. "On one condition." She glared at Holt. "I'm going, too."

In the end, Cody, Jessie and Devin all went and that was just fine with Holt.

"Everyone comfortable?" he asked.

Jessie, seated in the passenger seat of his truck, buckled her seat belt and nodded—the very same stoic expression she'd adopted a couple hours ago in Hummingbird Haven's community cabin when she'd announced she would be accompanying him on the trip for supplies as well.

"Yes." The forced smile on her face made Holt frown. She glanced over her shoulder at the boys, who sat in the backseat of his cab. "You guys comfortable back there?"

Cody grinned. "Yep."

Devin shrugged, leaned his elbow on the windowsill and propped his chin on his hand.

Holt looked in the rearview mirror, the sight of his sons sitting in the backseat so reminiscent of the night seven years ago when he'd nestled them in their car seats and driven to Hummingbird Haven. So many years had passed. He'd let them down so badly and had missed so much. So many milestone moments of his sons' lives that he would never be able to recapture.

How had he ever imagined reconnecting as a father with Cody and Devin after just an introduction and a few meaningful interactions? Jessie had been right. The risks associated with him reentering Cody and Devin's lives were high and he had no way of mitigating those risks without Jessie's help…and trust. Something she didn't seem too keen on offering him, despite what she'd said, given her less than enthusiastic response to him having a short outing with Cody and Devin.

Excitement fizzling, he forced a smile, too. "Well. Let's have a grocery store adventure, shall we?"

Cody laughed, Devin rolled his eyes and Jessie continued staring stoically ahead. Fifteen minutes later, the three of them surrounding him in the deodorant aisle of Hope Springs Family Grocery, their demeanors remained unchanged.

Seeking to break the ice, Holt grabbed a red container of deodorant, uncapped it and held it toward Cody's nose. "Now, this," he said, "*this* is deodorant made for a man."

Cody leaned in, took a big whiff and grinned. "Smells like pine."

"Uh-huh." Smiling, Holt turned to his right and offered it to Devin. "Outdoorsy. Full of a rich, woodsy, earthy type of scent."

Devin sniffed, an expression of reluctant approval in his eyes. "It does smell better."

A disgruntled sound emerged from Jessie's direction, but her lips twitched ever so slightly, giving Holt hope. "Are the three of you trying to say my deodorant stinks?"

Cody spread his hands. "Maybe."

Devin shook his head. "I didn't say that."

"What I'm saying," Holt clarified, "is that as delightful as the wildflowers are, I think this scent is better suited to me."

That lip twitch stretched into a full-blown smile. "You're delighted by my wildflowers?"

His neck heated. "No. I mean, I think it's nice on you."

A teasing light entered her eyes. "Really?"

He smiled—sincerely this time. That bit of humor in her tone was promising. Maybe this trip wouldn't be a complete dud. Maybe she'd give him a chance to show her that he could get along well with the boys *and* with her. "Yeah." He held her gaze. "Really."

Jessie's smile slipped, her cheeks flushing as she looked away. She headed for the exit, pausing briefly to say, "Boys, please help Mr. Holt pick out his supplies and I'll meet you at the truck."

The stiffness in her tone made Holt's stomach drop.

The drive back to Hummingbird Haven was silent. Jessie and Devin stared out their windows as the sun slowly began to set and Cody drifted off a time or two, waking himself up with a snore as Holt parked the truck in front of Jessie's cabin.

Holt helped Cody hop out of the truck and Jessie did the same for Devin.

"All right, boys," she said. "Let's get you washed up and ready for bed."

"Jessie?" Holt leaned against the bumper of his truck and waited for her to look back at him. "You mind staying behind a minute? Have something I need to ask you."

She hesitated then nodded. "Boys, why don't you go on in, brush your teeth and get your towels ready for your baths? I'll be in soon."

They complied, trudging up the steps and onto the porch where Cody stopped to wave at Holt.

"Bye, Mr. Holt." A sleepy smile crossed Cody's face. "Thanks for taking us to the store."

Holt smiled back, an intense longing rising within him as the boys headed inside the cabin. "You're welcome."

The screen door snapped shut behind them just as dusk fell and a chorus of tree frogs and crickets rolled along the tree line at the edge of the lawn. Cool air drifted in, prompting Jessie to cross her arms over her chest and rub her shoulders.

"So?" she asked, facing him. "What is it you want to ask me?"

Holt dragged his boot across the loose dirt of

the driveway, noting the space between them. "Why did you invite me to stay if you're so afraid of my being here?"

She bristled. "I'm not afraid of you."

"I think you are," he said softly. "This is day one and already, you're pushing me away. You got that arm of yours stretched out so stiff, I may never get past it."

Suspicion flashed in her eyes. "And why would you want to do that?"

"To get to know the boys." He shoved off his truck and stepped closer. "And you. I'd like to—no, I need to get to know you better. For the boys. For us."

She stepped back. "What us? I told you that—"

"You think I know you well enough already." He took another step, small rocks crunching under his boots. "But I don't. I know you're a great mom." He motioned toward the cabin where the boys were. "Anyone can see that. And I've known you were a great woman since the day I put my sons in your arms." He moved closer. "Look… I know I'm the furthest thing from perfect, but I'm not a bad guy and I'm trying here. I'm really trying. I just need to know when—or if—you're going to start trying, too."

"Try to do what?"

"Try to let that wall of yours down, open up a little and give me a chance with my boys. And maybe…" *Maybe with you?* He stopped walking, the thought catching him off guard, a deep longing unfurling in his chest. "You're a family," he said softly. "You and the boys. The only way I can truly become a part of the boys' lives here is if you let me in. I thought that's what you were trying to do by inviting me here, but you continue to push me away at every opportuni—"

"And why shouldn't I push you away? Because you say you've changed?" Her voice broke, the dying light of the setting sun glinting across a sheen of tears in her eyes. "Because now you say you're ready to be Cody and Devin's father?"

He shook his head, an exasperated sigh bursting from his lips. "I was just hoping—"

"I had plans." Two big tears broke free, dangled precariously on her long lashes for a moment, then plunged down her cheeks. "I've been here for Cody and Devin every moment of every day since you left them with me." A fresh set of tears coursed down her red cheeks. "I just applied for adoption. I was going to make it official—be their mother in every sense of the word—and then here you come.

Showing up at my door again, asking me to give them back to you. *My* sons."

Holt's throat tightened at the pained expression on her face.

"And what is it you're asking me to do?" she asked, a heavy sob racking her slender frame. "To trust that you've changed? To believe that it's okay to allow myself—and Cody and Devin—to be vulnerable to you? To put Cody and Devin at risk of being abandoned again like you abandoned them once before, like my mother abandoned me?"

He froze.

"You wanted to know more about me." She spoke softly. So softly he could barely hear. "So there it is. I didn't end up opening this shelter by chance. Years ago, hours after I was born, I was left behind like the children I offer shelter to here. Except my mother didn't hand me off to someone like you did Cody and Devin. She just left me in a parking lot like I was nothing of value. As though she didn't care if I was found alive or not. I spent my entire life in foster care. I've never had a family—not a real one. Certainly not the kind I plan to give Cody and Devin."

Eyes burning, he sucked in a strong breath. "Jessie—"

"Yes," she said. "I do think it's possible

you've changed. I do think you mean well... that you truly want to be a part of Cody and Devin's lives. But I'm afraid. I'm afraid of you getting close to Cody and Devin then changing your mind, leaving them again and breaking their hearts—like my mother broke mine the night she left me. But I'm even more afraid of things going well—of you keeping true to your word and becoming the father Cody and Devin deserve, the boys taking a shine to you...and wondering where that will leave me." She folded in on herself, her head lowering, arms wrapping around her waist and tears flowing freely. "Allowing you in is scarier than you think. And it's harder than you could ever imagine."

"Jessie..." Heart clenching, he moved slowly to her side. Lifted a shaky hand and touched her arm. "Jessie."

She raised her head then, met his eyes and held his gaze, tears pooling in the corners of her trembling mouth as she studied his face. Then, slowly—so very slowly—she stepped forward and touched her forehead to his chest, her words barely discernable as she said, "I'll try. I promise I'll start trying."

Instinctively, his arms lifted, but he halted his movements, forced his hands to still in mid-air and hover inches from her back, afraid to intrude more than he already had. He lowered his head and breathed in the sweet scent of her hair, fighting his desperate desire to wrap her safely in his arms and hold her close, trying to be patient and give her the space she needed instead.

"I know," he whispered, allowing his lips to barely brush the top of her head. "I know."

Chapter Nine

God had a reason for everything. Jessie truly believed that—at least, that was what she told herself as she stood outside Creek Cabin at six o'clock the next morning.

It was dark out, the spring sun still snoozing, and only a few lavender tendrils of light unfurled along the mountain range in the distance. A lone bird chirped from the depths of a thick Cypress tree and a chilly breeze rustled through thick branches and swept across the clearing, coaxing goose bumps along Jessie's bare arms.

Jessie tugged the short sleeves of her T-shirt down a bit, shoved her hands into the pockets of her jeans and bounced in place. "Shoulda brought a jacket," she mumbled to herself as she eyed the front door of Creek Cabin.

She should've brought a lot of things and left

others behind. Take her pride, for instance. She could've left that at home in favor of a light windbreaker. It would've made this endeavor a whole lot less painful. But then again, in her experience, eating crow was never a very pleasant experience under any circumstances.

And maybe that's the problem, a little voice chimed inside her head.

She made a face. Perhaps it was. Maybe her conscience had a point. Maybe apologizing to Holt for her emotional outburst last night and taking the first step to openly invite him into her and the boys' lives only seemed like an insurmountable task because the act itself proved one thing above all: she had been pushing him away as a result of her own fears and insecurities—unfairly, as he'd suggested—despite offering to help him reconnect with Cody and Devin. And she'd allowed it to all spill out in a tearful tirade last night.

A light flickered on above the tiny window of the cabin's kitchen. Holt, clad in a short-sleeved T-shirt and jeans, ambled into view and stretched one muscular arm upward to the left of the window.

He was probably rooting around in one of the cabinets for a mug. Jessie lifted her shoulders toward her ears and stamped her feet, fighting off the early-morning chill. A hot cup of coffee would be more than welcome right about now and clearly, Holt was up and about now, which left her no more excuses as to why she should delay the inevitable.

Oh, buck up, girl, that annoying voice chimed. *You promised him last night that you'd try. So apologize and...try.*

Sighing, she squared her shoulders, marched up to the front door and knocked twice.

The door opened a moment later and Holt, surprise in his eyes, surveyed her silently for a moment then stepped back and swept his arm toward the interior of the cabin. "Please, come in."

She did so, saying as she stepped across the threshold, "Thank you. I hate to bother you so early but..." She glanced around, eyes flicking nervously over the familiar features of the living room. "Um, Zoe and the boys are fixing a big breakfast at her cabin and we wanted to invite you over to eat with the boys and see them off to school this morning." She withdrew a small piece of paper from her back pocket. "And I made a list—like you mentioned yesterday—of the to-dos we need done around the property so you'll know what to expect for the next few workdays." She rubbed at a speck of ink on her thumb, left behind from the pen she used to compose the list before walking to Creek Cabin. "I also wanted to talk to you before we started work for the day, if that's okay?"

"Always."

The warm tone of his voice stilled the nervous flutters in her stomach. She refocused on his face and her gaze fixated on a lock of blond hair that had fallen over his left eye. It caught on his dark lashes, moving as he blinked. Her fingers itched to reach up and smooth it back. Maybe take a step forward and lean her cheek against his strong, warm chest as she had last night.

But that would be a mistake—one she couldn't afford. His physical attraction...well, she'd become pretty adept at fending that off, but his tenderness—the kind he'd shown her last night with his patient demeanor, soothing tone and comforting presence—that was much more difficult to ignore.

She'd dated in the past—though having dedicated most of her time to Hummingbird Haven the dates had been few—but none of the men she'd dated had stirred the intense emotions in her that Holt did. The feelings she experienced for him were an odd new mixture of tenderness, excitement...and dismay for how deeply he affected her. She was used to being in control of her surroundings and emotions, and Holt's presence evoked a vulnerability in her she hadn't expected.

He shoved his hair off his forehead, revealing an unobstructed view of the kindness in his hazel eyes. "I'm always available anytime you'd like to talk and I'd love to have breakfast with the boys." He glanced at the list then put it in his pocket and smiled. "And thank you for the to-do list. It'll help me manage my time better."

The sculpted curves of his mouth caught her attention, his soft words seeming to linger in her ears and on his parted lips as she stared.

She shook her head, stepped back and resumed surveying the living room again.

Gurgling sounds emerged from the kitchen.

"I just made a fresh pot of coffee," he said. "Would you like some while we talk?"

Grateful for the distraction, she managed a smile. "Yes, please."

He led the way into the kitchen where the aroma of freshly ground coffee beans hovered on the air. One white mug sat on the laminate countertop by the coffeemaker and after grabbing another from a cabinet beside the kitchen window, he picked up the carafe and filled each mug to an inch from the rim with coffee.

"I picked up some milk and sugar last night

at the store," he said over his shoulder. "Would you like both?"

"Please."

"You like it dark or light?"

"Light and heavy on the sugar."

He smiled. "You got it."

Once he'd doctored one mug with milk and a heaping spoonful of sugar, he cradled the mug in his big hand and offered it to her.

She took it from him, trying to ignore the way his warm fingers brushed against hers, then took a sip and made a sound of appreciation. "It's perfect. Thank you."

"You're welcome." He leaned against the counter and brought his own mug to his lips, eyeing her expectantly over the rim as he sipped.

"I…" She drank another quick swig of coffee and winced as the hot liquid scorched her throat on the way down. "I'd like to apologize for my behavior last night. I should've been more receptive with Cody's request to go shopping with you, and I should've encouraged their interest in you rather than trying to discourage it. That is, after all, the reason I invited you here."

He lowered his mug, and her gaze was drawn to the strong column of his throat as he swallowed.

"A—and I'm sorry for my outburst last night," she added. "I didn't mean to dump my baggage on you like that. Especially when we already have enough to carry what with figuring out how Cody and Devin's future will look."

Brow creasing, he looked down, tapped his blunt fingertips against his mug then met her eyes again. "I'm glad you told me. I expected my return to be difficult for you, but I didn't realize just how difficult. I can't imagine how painful this must be for you."

It didn't sound like a question, but she answered him honestly anyway.

"Yeah. It's not exactly easy." She wrapped both of her palms around her mug, attempting to still the tremor running through them. "Though I don't think this situation is any easier for you, either, especially after I compared your behavior with my mother's—which I shouldn't have, by the way. You took great care to protect Cody and Devin and I shouldn't have made things so personal last night."

"But this is personal," he said quietly. "It's very personal for both of us, isn't it?"

She stared at her mug, watched two small bubbles float around the creamy brown surface of the liquid, then nodded.

"I'm glad you told me," he said. "And there's no need to apologize."

Acutely aware of his gaze, she drank another sip of coffee and cringed as heat suffused her face.

"Jessie?"

She licked her lips, the sweet taste hitting her tongue, then forced herself to meet his eyes.

"I'm in this for the long haul and have no intention of leaving my sons again. And I know how hard that is for you to believe." He set his mug on the counter and moved closer, dipping his blond head to level his gaze with hers. "But I also know—all legalities aside—that you are, always have been, and always will be, their mother. I know how much Cody and Devin love you," he continued, "and how much I…"

Breath catching, she parted her lips and inhaled, the spicy scent of his aftershave rushing in, filling her senses. His broad chest was close enough that his warmth drifted over to her, bringing to mind the remembered feel of his solid strength beneath her forehead last night, how comforting and protective his presence had felt.

She studied his expression as his eyes roved over her face. "How much you what?"

"How much I care about you as well."

Her hands tightened around her mug, the hot ceramic cup almost burning her palms as a bittersweet sensation stirred in her middle. "You c-care about me?"

"Yeah." His eyes met hers again, darkening as a slow smile lifted the corners of his mouth. "Even though you weren't aware of it, you've been a part of my life for seven years. I've admired you from afar. Thought about you every day, just as I have my sons. I've never forgotten what you did for my sons that night—or for me. And I've thanked God every day for you answering the door. For offering compassion instead of turning me away and for providing me the opportunity now to get to know my sons again. Your kindness and generosity are part of what prompted me to change, to wish I could be as good a person as you."

That bittersweet feeling vanished. She stared down at her coffee again. "Oh."

He appreciated her as a good person…but not as a woman. Her stomach sank. Perhaps her attraction to him was one-sided. Maybe she didn't stir the same emotions in him that he evoked in her?

His hands curved around hers, his callused palms settling over the backs of her hands, coaxing her eyes back up to meet his. "I would never—ever—even think of taking Cody and

Devin out of your life. No matter how we end up working this out, you will always be their mother, and you will always be entitled to that role in their lives. I hope I can at least put that fear to rest."

She held his gaze for a moment, the sincerity in his words and expression unmistakable… but not exactly what she wanted to hear. "You might not take them out of my life but you'd still consider taking them out of my home, wouldn't you?"

His earnest expression fell, and he slowly removed his hands from hers. "I won't lie to you, Jessie. There's nothing I want more than to have my sons with me again on a permanent basis. So yes. For me, the ideal outcome of this situation would be to resume my role as their father and take my sons home to my family in Pine Creek—for good."

Jessie walked to the kitchen counter, set her mug down beside Holt's and dragged a hand through her hair. "And, for me, the ideal outcome would be adopting Cody and Devin and keeping them here at Hummingbird Haven with me. Which leaves us at an impasse." She turned back to face him. "Still."

Holt turned his head and looked out the kitchen window, a pensive expression on his face. "But at least we know where we stand

and it's up to us to carve a new path out of this standstill we've reached." He refocused on her, his eyes locking with hers. "I hope what I've shared with you will help you understand my intentions better."

Oh, sure. She nodded slowly, studying his thick rumpled hair, the light stubble lining his jaw and the strong curves of his brawny form. He saw her as some self-sacrificing, matronly figure of the past whose high standards and dedication to his sons had cemented an obligation in his mind to do right by her. To work with her in an honest and forthright manner for the boys' sake. *Our boys*, as he'd referenced Cody and Devin last night.

Sincerity had been ingrained in every inch of his being as he'd shared his thoughts with her, and every bit of it sounded great—exactly the type of candid, respectful approach that would be expected from a man who claimed he'd changed. So why did his every word leave her feeling deflated and…empty?

She stole one last moment, admiring the handsome features of his face, as she summoned her most professional tone, the meaning of his words that left her feeling hollow fully sinking in. "Yes," she said. "Everything you do will be done in the best interest of your sons. Solely for Cody and Devin's sake."

* * *

It had to be the company but Holt had never tasted pancakes as scrumptious as the ones Cody and Devin plopped on his plate at the kitchen table in Zoe's cabin—even after Cody submerged them in two inches of syrup.

"Mmm." Holt forked another saturated hunk into his mouth, his eyes watering when 100 percent pure maple sugar coated his sensitive teeth, but he smiled anyway, the sweetness of the moment shooting straight to his heart. "These are the best pancakes I've ever had in my life."

Cody, now seated in a chair beside Holt at the table, beamed. "We made 'em special. Ms. Zoe let me add cinnamon to the batter even though Devin didn't want it."

"You're s'posed to use cinnamon at Thanksgiving," Devin grumbled. He sat on the other side of Cody and eyed his empty plate with disdain. "That's when Jessie always uses it."

"So?" Cody pointed at Devin's empty plate. "You ate 'em all so you must've liked them."

Devin shrugged. "Yeah, I guess."

Holt ate the last bite of his pancake and patted his middle. "That was some good eating, boys." He glanced at Miles, who sat at the other end of the table, still nibbling on his last pancake. "What about you, Miles? Did you enjoy the pancakes?"

Miles glanced up, meeting Holt's eyes for a moment, then quickly looked back down and nodded.

Well, that was an improvement at least.

After his conversation with Jessie, he'd walked with her along one of the trails to Zoe's cabin. It had been a nice, but quiet, stroll as Jessie had responded to his few polite attempts at chitchat with mute nods and smiles. Eventually, he'd fallen silent, too, lulled into the same type of contemplative reflection Jessie seemed to have undertaken and had focused instead on the rays of the rising sun as they spilled slowly through the treetops and dappled the dirt trail with patches of light and shadow.

When they'd reached Zoe's cabin, Zoe, Cody and Devin had welcomed them in with big smiles and excited fanfare but Miles, whom Holt assumed lived with Zoe, had sat silently at the kitchen table, his wide eyes following each of Holt's movements. Miles had ignored Holt's greeting and hadn't spoken throughout breakfast, so Holt decided to count the nod as progress.

"I know I enjoyed them." Zoe, standing at the kitchen sink, loading dirty dishes into the dishwasher, groaned good-naturedly as she rubbed her belly. "The bacon, too. I ate enough to hibernate through the winter. But, boy, was it tasty." Wincing, she set the dirty plate she held back into the sink and picked at her teeth. "And I'll probably have a cavity by morning."

Holt laughed, stood and started stacking the dirty dishes left at the table. "I know what you mean. I take it y'all stockpile syrup somewhere on the premises?"

Zoe grinned. "Better. Our closest—well, pretty much only—neighbor, Brent Cason, makes his own. He doesn't usually sell it, but I talked him into making a few bottles for us every year."

Jessie, sipping coffee as she stood by the kitchen table, raised her brows at Zoe. "Bribed him, you mean?"

Zoe spread her hands with an innocent expression. "All I did was make him an offer he couldn't refuse."

"Yeah…okay," Jessie said. "You best give Brent a wide berth. He's not keen on visitors."

Zoe's grin dimmed. "He's not keen on much of anything as far as I can tell."

There was something in her voice—a hint of longing and disappointment. The same despondent tone that had laced Jessie's words earlier in Holt's cabin. He recognized it immediately.

Holt glanced at Jessie, who'd turned her attention to the kitchen window, silently gazing out at the scenic beauty of the mountain range. Something had shifted between them.

She'd surprised him with her visit this morning and the small leap of eager excitement within him at the sight of her standing at his door hadn't escaped his notice. Now aware of her past, he'd grown more appreciative of her allowing him into Cody and Devin's lives. She could've so easily turned him away, but she'd decided to continue, to try to let him in even when it was painful for her.

He respected her all the more for it…and he hoped that the slight tinge of disappointment in her tone when she'd acknowledged he was here solely for the boys might have been a reflection of her softening toward him. That maybe, after allowing herself to lean on him last night, she'd begun to feel the same stirring of affection for him. Maybe she wasn't quite as unaffected by him as a man as he'd assumed. And maybe, given time, she'd grow to trust him as a man and not just as Cody and Devin's father.

He pulled his gaze away from her. That wasn't the reason he was here, he reminded himself firmly. He was here for Cody and Devin—not to explore his attraction to Jessie, no matter how honorable his intentions might be.

"Here, let me get that for you." Holt joined Zoe at the sink and started loading the dirty plates into the sink. "You and the boys worked so hard cooking breakfast, the least I can do is take care of the dirty dishes. And maybe I could return the favor and cook a meal for you, Jessie and the boys one day?"

Zoe's grin returned, complete with a look of impressed admiration. "Oh, I think I'm gonna like having you around." She glanced at Jessie as she strolled around him, nodding. "Yep. I could definitely get used to this kind of help."

Holt chuckled. Zoe's good mood and easygoing nature were infectious. "That's good to hear." He glanced at Cody, Devin and Miles, who still sat at the kitchen table, eyeing him with curiosity. "Lesson number one on being a gentleman, boys. Never leave a lady in the kitchen alone with dirty dishes. It doesn't matter who cooks. If you eat, you clean."

The trio nodded solemnly.

"Wanna give me a hand?" Holt asked.

Cody sprang to his feet and Devin followed his brother, joining Holt at the sink. Miles walked over to Zoe's side and watched from afar.

"How many lessons does it take to be a gentleman?" Cody asked, grabbing a handful of dirty forks and loading them into the dishwasher.

"As many as it takes," Holt said.

Devin picked up the dirty plate Zoe had placed in the sink. He looked up at Holt, a cautious look in his eyes. "Will you teach us some of them? Or all of them?"

Holt stared down at Devin, his blond hair, tanned cheeks and stubborn chin so like his own when he was a boy. But the look in Devin's hazel eyes—that untrusting wariness—Holt had put that there seven years ago.

Throat closing, Holt reached out and ruffled Devin's hair gently. Then, glancing at Jessie, who watched him with the same expression, he said, "Jessie and I will teach you all of them together, if that's okay with you?"

Devin considered this, watching warily as Holt withdrew his hand and lowered it to his side. "Yeah," he said, glancing at Cody. "I guess that'd be okay."

Cody squealed. "When's lesson two?"

"Right now," Jessie said, striding over. "It's time to load up in Zoe's van, and gentlemen are sometimes early but never late. Finish up with the dishes then grab your bookbags."

Ten minutes later Holt stood at the end of the driveway with Jessie, Cody and Devin standing between them as Zoe warmed the engine of Hummingbird Haven's colorful van.

Cody hitched his bookbag higher on his back and smiled up at Holt. "When will lesson three be? This afternoon after school? Are you gonna have snack time with us again? Help us with our homework? Can we go shopping with you again?"

Holt laughed as he held up a hand. "Hold up, there. There's no need to rush through anything. And yes, I'll have snack time with y'all again after school if that's okay with Jessie?"

She smoothed her hand through Devin's hair, straightening a few strands Holt had ruffled earlier. "Of course. Mr. Holt will be pitching in all over while he's here. And his first order of business is—"

"To fix the back deck at Creek Cabin." Holt tugged the to-do list from his back pocket and scanned the tasks Jessie had written. "I'll need to pick up decking boards and I thought I'd apply some stain, if that works for you? I think a dark stain would help it blend in with the surrounding woodland better and give it a more aesthetic appeal. I could pick up supplies this morning and start on the deck this afternoon."

"Sounds good," Jessie said. "I have an account with the hardware store in town where

Peggy Ann works. I'll call the manager and let him know you're coming."

"Can I help you fix the deck?" Cody asked, tugging Holt's wrist. "I can carry a deck board for you."

Holt smiled. "Thank you. I'd love the help."

Zoe, seated in the driver's seat of the van, leaned out the open window and motioned at Cody and Devin. "Come on, guys, everyone's loaded up but you and it's time to go."

"For now," Holt told Cody, "I think it's best you board the van like Zoe asked and focus on your schoolwork. Lesson number three," he said, holding up three fingers. "A gentleman is dedicated to doing his best work—no matter the task at hand."

Smiling wide, Cody skipped over, threw his arms around Holt's waist and squeezed. "I will, Mr. Holt. I promise."

Breath catching, Holt blinked against the tears pricking at the backs of his eyes and hugged Cody back, the realization of his son being in his arms for the first time in seven years overwhelming him, even though Cody's hug was meant for a stranger—not his father.

The moment ended too soon.

"Bye, Mr. Holt!" Cody had already sprung away and bolted up into the backseat of the van, following Devin, who'd already boarded.

"Bye, guys!" Jessie called, waving. "Have a great day at school."

Cody, Devin and Miles waved back from the windows of the van as Zoe drove away.

Holt frowned. "Peggy Ann's girls don't ride with Zoe to school?"

Jessie remained silent for a moment. "They usually do. But Peggy Ann decided to drive them to school herself this morning on the way to the hardware store." She fidgeted, picking at her fingernails. "I think she wanted some alone time with them. Or maybe just—"

"There's no need to explain," Holt said. "I picked up on the fact that meeting me last night must've been unexpected and possibly unwelcome for her and her daughters."

Her hand touched his forearm, her fingers laying gently against his skin. "It's not you, Holt. It's the idea of a stranger—a man—she doesn't know being so close. She just came out of an abusive relationship. She has doubts."

Holt moved, took her hand in his, cradling her graceful fingers gently as he met her eyes, the cautious uncertainty in her gaze wounding him as deeply as Devin's had. "I know," he whispered. "We all do."

Chapter Ten

"What do you mean they don't know who you are?"

Holt frowned at the recrimination in Liam's tone, palmed the steering wheel of his truck and turned, guiding the vehicle into the parking lot of Bennett & Sons Hardware. After parking, he unhooked his cell phone from the dashboard mount and sighed.

"What I mean," Holt said, "is that neither Cody nor Devin—nor any of the rest of the residents—know I'm their father. Only Jessie and her partner, Zoe, know who I am and why I'm really there."

The voice on the other end of the line was silent for a moment, then, "And you signed up for this? You got to be kidding me, Holt."

Liam was not happy.

"Look," Holt said, cutting the truck's engine.

"The reason Jessie suggested we do things this way was—"

"To take advantage of the situation—*and you*." A frustrated growl crossed the line. "Don't you see what she's doing? She's keeping you boxed in a corner right under her nose and throwing you a scrap now and then to keep you content long enough to come up with a reason to get rid of you. She has no intention of letting you close to your s—"

"Cody hugged me this morning." The words caught in Holt's throat, emotion overwhelming him again. Blinking hard, he stared out the windshield at the entrance of the hardware store, watching as an elderly couple, holding hands, strolled inside. "Granted, he didn't know he was hugging *me* instead of a stranger, but he actually hugged me. And all I could think about was how good it felt to have my son in my arms again. How I should never have let them go to begin with and how much I have to make up for."

"Holt—"

"No." Holt shifted in his seat, sitting taller. "Jessie didn't coerce me into agreeing to anything. I knew what I was getting into. I trust Jessie. She's been a great mom to my sons and more than accommodating to me, given the circumstances."

"Okay," Liam said quietly. "Am I allowed to ask what these circumstances are?"

"The shelter she runs isn't just for abandoned children," Holt said. "It's for abused women, too. From what I've witnessed and heard, Jessie's worked hard for a long time to make Hummingbird Haven a safe place for these women and children, and she has every right to protect them—even from me. I'm abiding by her wishes for now."

Liam grew quiet again. "Is there something else going on here?" His tone altered. Turned hesitant. "Something more going on between you and Jessie you wanna tell me about?"

Holt stilled, a slight smile tugging at his mouth. "You've never been one to beat around the bush, have you?"

His deep chuckle sounded in Holt's ear. "You know me well."

"As well as I hope you know me now," Holt said, his smile fading as he thought of Jessie. How loving and protective she was of his sons…and how vulnerable she was in all of this. "In the past, I never shied away from being attracted to a woman, but things are different now. What I feel for Jessie is different. Going into this, I knew I admired her, that I was grateful to her for all she did for me and Cody and Devin, and I never expected to feel something more than that. But I do—more and more every day. Thing is, there couldn't be a worse time or place to feel what I'm feeling, and I don't want anything to jeopardize what might be my only chance to be a part of Cody and Devin's lives."

Liam was quiet for a moment then asked, "Have you spoken to her about how you're feeling?"

"No." Holt shook his head, his gut sinking at the memory of the wary look in her eyes when they'd spoken last night. "She's dealing with as much as—if not more than—I am right now and, besides, I can't even put a name yet to what I'm feeling." He shook his head again, dismissing the notion. "No. It's better to keep things as they are for now. To just focus on Cody and Devin and their future to the exclusion of everything else."

Silence lingered across the line, then Liam said, "Okay. I told you I'd support you and that's what I'll do. I'm just a call away if you need to talk. And, Holt?"

"Yeah?"

"Mom asked if she'll be able to see the boys sometime soon. And you. She misses you." His tone softened. "She knows you've changed—she has no doubts about that—but she lost so many years with you when you left with Dad that she gets a bit antsy when she doesn't see you occasionally."

Holt closed his eyes and rubbed his eyelids. "I know. I'm working on coming home and bringing the boys for a visit, but it may take a while. Just…would you please ask her to be patient and trust me?" He paused. "And you, too, Liam?"

He answered without hesitation. "You got it, brother."

Holt said goodbye and ended the call, put his cell phone in his pocket and entered the hardware store. As expected, Peggy Ann stood by a cash register behind a large counter in the center of the store.

"Good morning, Peggy Ann." Holt approached the counter slowly, stopped in front of Peggy Ann and placed his hands flat on the counter. "I spoke with Jessie this morning about needing to pick up deck boards and stain to repair the deck at Creek Cabin. She said she was going to call the manager and let him know I'd be swinging by to pick up supplies."

She smiled, though it seemed strained, and nodded. "Yes. She called and Mr. Bancroft, our manager, and one of our other employees are rounding up what you need." She hesitated, her gaze skittering away from his. "I'm sorry about the wait. I was hoping they'd have it ready to load by the time you made it here."

"It's okay," he said gently, trying his best to put her at ease in his presence. "There's no rush at all. As a matter of fact, I was hoping to take care of something else while I was in town. Would it be okay if I left and came back in about an hour or so?"

Peggy Ann's polite smile returned, her shoulders seeming to sag with relief. "Of course. If you'd like to leave your number, I could text you when everything's ready."

Holt smiled back. "That'd be great. Thank you."

She handed him a notepad and pen and as he wrote his cell number down, he felt her intense gaze on him. He slid the pad back to her.

"When you come back," she said, gesturing toward the back of the store, "just pull around to the loading dock and Mr. Bancroft will have someone load everything up for you."

"Thank you, Peggy Ann. I really appreciate it." He headed for the exit.

"Mr…er, Holt?"

He stopped, glancing over his shoulder.

Peggy Ann stared back at him. Her mouth opened and closed twice before she said, "I'd like to welcome you to Hummingbird Haven.

I…uh, I don't think I told you that yesterday when we met."

Holt nodded. "That's okay," he said gently. "And thank you for that."

"I know Jessie and Zoe are grateful to have your help around the place." Some of the tension left her expression and she smiled once more before returning her attention to a stack of invoices and a laptop that sat next to the cash register.

Holt's smile grew, his chest lifting just a bit with a newfound sense of pride at the thought of being helpful. Of easing someone else's burdens. Of contributing to a valuable cause, the likes of which he'd never engaged with before.

He was still smiling as he returned to his truck, cranked the engine and drove away.

Fifteen minutes later Holt exited an elevator and walked onto the top floor of Hope Springs Hospital where he and Jessie had visited the Boarder Baby Unit days earlier.

"You're back." Surprise lit Nurse Sharon's eyes as she sat behind the welcome desk.

Holt nodded. He hadn't expected to turn off the main road into town and park in the hospital lot, but that feeling of pride he'd felt minutes earlier in the hardware store still lingered, and when he'd spotted the hospital, he'd thought of Ava, alone in her nursery crib, and he'd acted automatically, parking his truck and going inside.

"Jessie isn't with me today." He walked up to the welcome desk and smiled. "I'm running an errand in town and have some time to kill, so I thought I'd check and see if it's okay if I visit Ava on my own."

Sharon tilted her head, her gaze roving over him for a moment, then lifted her shoulders. "Well, I don't see why not. You were cleared with a background check for your original visit, and it would just take one more signature to put you on the list as an official volunteer." A perplexed expression crossed her face. "Is that what you're asking? If you can volunteer?"

"Yes, please." Holt withdrew his wallet from his back pocket and produced his license. "I have my ID, too, in case you needed it again."

Nodding, Sharon accepted his driver's license and smiled. "Thanks. I'll just grab the paperwork."

Five minutes later Holt's name had been officially added to the volunteer list. He was, as he had requested, assigned to Ava.

Sharon glanced at her watch. "It's almost time for her next feeding. Would you like to take up where you left off the other day?"

"That sounds good. Thank you."

Holt followed Sharon down the familiar hallway and into Ava's room. The room was the same as before, cheerfully decorated and peaceful. Small babbling sounds emerged from the crib.

"She's been a hungry girl the past day or two." Sharon peeked into the crib and smiled. "Haven't you, beautiful?"

Holt joined Sharon and leaned in, smiling as Ava's big blue eyes found him and widened as she studied his face. "How long does it take for a baby her age to recognize someone?"

"Oh, it depends. Babies her age tend to recognize individuals they spend a fair amount of time with. Feedings, diaper changes, cuddle sessions, they all add up over time."

He leaned closer, smiling as he returned Ava's stare. "So if I were to come every day and feed Ava at my lunch break and sit with her every evening, she'd begin to recognize me?"

Sharon didn't answer. She shifted beside him, her hand curling around the crib rail near where his own hand lay. "May I ask what motivated you to come here today? On your own, I mean. Without Jessie."

Holt straightened and faced her, hoping his sincerity showed in his expression. "I've made mistakes in my past. I assume Jessie has filled you in on some of the details of our current arrangement?"

"A bit," Sharon said softly. "But she didn't mention you'd be coming by to check on Ava. Is that why you're here? Because Jessie asked you to come?"

Holt shook his head. "No. This was my decision. I'd like to be the best version of the man I think I should be—the man I hope I already am. And I want to make a difference. I want to do some good to make up for the mistakes I've made. The kind I'll never be able to fully amend with my own sons. I don't want Ava to feel alone like my sons did. I want her to know that someone's thinking of her, that someone cares about her."

Sharon smiled, then gestured toward the rocking chair next to the crib. "Have a seat. I'll get Ava's bottle."

Holt did as she directed, glancing up at her as she reentered the room, a bottle in one hand and a metal folding chair clutched in the other.

"Bottle's warm and I brought a burping cloth," she said, placing them in his hands. "You remember how this goes?"

Nodding, Holt tossed the burping cloth over his shoulder, positioned the crook of his arm and held the bottle ready in his right hand.

Sharon lifted Ava from her crib and placed

her gently in his arms. Ava squirmed, her face scrunching up, as Holt settled her into a more comfortable position within his arms.

"Hi, beautiful," he whispered, tilting the bottle and bringing the nipple close to her rosebud mouth. "You hungry?"

Eyes wide, Ava latched on hard, drawing deeply from the bottle, her hungry sighs breaking the silence in the room as Sharon sat in the folding chair opposite him.

"It seems easier this time, huh?" Sharon asked quietly, crossing her ankles and easing back into her chair.

Holt smiled, keeping a careful grip on the bottle, and his muscles relaxed under Ava's delicate head and neck. "Yeah, a bit."

Holt stilled, a shaft of pain cutting deep into his chest as he stared down at Ava and thought of Jessie as a vulnerable infant, alone in the cold, crying as someone who should've loved and protected her walked away.

Tears pricked at the backs of his eyes. He blinked hard then stared down at baby Ava. No wonder Jessie's disdain—and distrust—for him ran so deep. He'd abandoned Cody and Devin just as Jessie's parents had abandoned her.

"What will happen to Ava?" he asked softly.

Sharon issued a sad smile. "Well, a search

is being conducted for her mother but the authorities who are investigating her case haven't discovered her yet. Neither Ava's father nor any other relatives have come forward, either. If nothing changes, she'll be placed in foster care until she's either adopted or ages out at eighteen."

"But..." Holt glanced at Ava, who still pulled steadily from the bottle. "Isn't it almost a guarantee that she'll be adopted? I was under the impression that infants were usually adopted more easily than older children."

"They are," Sharon said. "But in cases like Ava's, well...the circumstances surrounding a child's abandonment will sometimes dissuade a potential adoptive parent from following through. Sometimes, there are fears—mostly unfounded—that there may be some psychological or emotional damage down the road due to the nature of the abandonment. Or there are other fears such as the mother having an alcohol or drug addiction and the effects passing on to the fetus."

I spent my entire life in foster care. I've never had a family—not a real one.

Holt stilled, pain engulfing him as he recalled Jessie's words from last night and thought of her as a child, alone, with no family. No child should ever feel as though they weren't valuable or loved.

Sharon looked at Ava, her eyes glistening. "That's why Jessie works so hard to keep Hummingbird Haven and—" she gestured toward their surroundings "—this Boarder Baby Unit an integral part of our community. She does everything she can to remove the stigma surrounding the babies we care for as well as the women she shelters on her property. She believes everyone's entitled to a fair shot and fresh start in life no matter where they began."

"Everyone?" Holt considered this, wondering if Jessie's support might extend to someone like him—a man who'd left his sons just as Jessie's mom had left her. A man who'd caused many of his own unfortunate circumstances. Then he asked, "Even someone like me?"

Ava's movements in Holt's arms had slowed. Her eyes had grown heavy, and her thick lashes lowered to her rosy cheeks as her mouth slackened, releasing the bottle.

Holt set the bottle to the side, carefully lifted Ava to his shoulder and rubbed her back gently, a brief grin crossing his lips as a small burp sounded near his ear.

Sharon smiled as she studied him, watching his hand rub slow circles over Ava's back. "Given time and opportunity? Yes. I believe so."

* * *

Jessie, kneeling on the back deck of Creek Cabin, turned a pry bar over in her hands and trailed her fingers along the metal, recalling the gentle touch of Holt's hand cradling hers hours earlier as she'd shared that Peggy Ann had doubts.

We all do, he'd said, acknowledging he was aware of the struggle she'd undertaken inviting him into Cody and Devin's lives and taking a chance on trusting him. He'd been so patient and compassionate this morning, not for one moment making her feel embarrassed or uncomfortable about sharing her pain over her mother's abandonment or fears of his return into Cody and Devin's lives.

Holt had been every bit the gentleman he was teaching Cody, Devin and Miles to be.

She tapped her fingernail against the pry bar and closed her eyes as a swift spring breeze rippled through the trees and over the creek rushing alongside the deck, the *whoosh* of fresh, cool afternoon air sweeping over her.

It was silly—and surprising, really—that she'd begun fixating on Holt's voice, his words, his brief tender touches, instead of what was most important—Cody and Devin. Ever since Holt had left Hummingbird Haven and driven his truck out of the driveway and up the winding mountain road out of sight to pick up supplies for the deck repairs, she'd thought of little else but him.

Holt—and his intentions—had been on her mind as she'd called the hardware store and asked the manager to charge the supplies to her bill. She'd thought of Holt as she'd washed and dried a load of Cody and Devin's laundry, her fingers stilling on their small shirts when she'd folded them as her mind had drifted off again. And when the boys had returned from school an hour ago, hopped off the van, scarfed down their snacks and followed Holt eagerly to the Creek Cabin to begin repairs, she'd caught herself recalling his words from early that morning, the same hollow gaping in her stomach as she reminded herself why Holt had changed from the man he was and returned in the first place.

Solely for Cody and Devin's sakes.

"Lesson number four of being a gentleman." Holt, crouching next to her on the deck, motioned toward Cody, Devin and Miles, who stood by the back door of Creek Cabin. "You should always offer a helping hand to someone when they're working on a project and accept their wishes if they decline the help and prefer to complete the task on their own." His left biceps, bare below the short sleeve of his T-shirt, brushed her arm as he turned to the side to face the boys. "It'd be great if one of you offered Jessie some help with removing the rotten deck boards."

Cody's voice rang out. "But I want to help you with the joyces."

Jessie grinned, the mistake a welcome distraction from Holt's presence. "You mean joists," she said, scooting an inch away from Holt, just enough to evade the brush of his smooth muscle against her upper arm. She looked up at Cody. "You want to help Mr. Holt repair the joists."

"It's called sistering," Devin said, lifting his chin at Holt. "Isn't that what you said?"

Holt nodded, a gleam of pride lighting his eyes. "That's exactly right, Devin." He tilted his head and whispered to Jessie, "He has a good head on his shoulders, yeah?"

Jessie nodded. "He's very advanced for his age. Gifted, they think. Cody is much more extroverted and very inquisitive."

"Sistering?" Cody repeated, scrunching his nose as his eyes widened. "Hey. You got a sister, Mr. Holt?"

Holt laughed. "No, I don't."

"What about a brother?" Cody asked.

"I've got one of those," Holt said.

"Is he younger or older than you?" Cody asked.

"Older."

"How much older?"

Holt grinned. "One minute."

"One minute?" Cody tilted his head and frowned then... "Wait!" Excitement shined in his eyes. "You got a twin? Like me and Devin?"

Jessie looked at Holt, his gaze meeting hers. He shifted his weight from one foot to the other as she slowly shook her head, then returned his attention to Cody.

"Yeah." His gaze settled on Devin, who stared back at him. "I have a twin brother."

"A twin?" Devin repeated.

Oh no. Jessie set the pry bar down and eased back on her haunches. She could almost hear the wheels turning in Devin's advanced young mind.

Devin frowned. "He has blond hair, too?"

"Yes," Holt said.

Devin's eyes narrowed. "You look the same? Identical, like me and Cody?"

Holt nodded.

"Devin." Jessie scrambled to her feet and jogged to Devin's side, carefully sidestepping two rotten deck boards. "I could really use your help. How about you and I grab a plastic bag from the kitchen?" She glanced at Holt.

"I assume there are still a couple in one of the kitchen drawers?" At Holt's nod, she placed her hands on Devin's shoulders and steered him through the back door of the cabin. "And you can sit with me while I remove the rotten deck boards and you can collect the old nails and screws for me. That way none of them will end up on the deck for someone's bare feet to step on in the summer."

Devin's frown deepened but he complied, allowing her to lead him through the cabin and into the kitchen.

"Now," she said as she opened a drawer by the sink, "where do I remember seeing those plastic bags?"

"Jessie?"

She closed the drawer and opened another. "Hmm?"

"He has a twin."

No bags here, either. She shoved the drawer shut, walked across the kitchen and opened another, turning her back to Devin. "Yep, he does."

"And he has blond hair."

She sifted through another drawer.

"Like me and Cod—"

"Found one!" Jessie snatched up a clear plastic bag, spun back to Devin and waved it high in the air. "This will work perfectly. All you need to do is drop the nails and screws in the bag when I hand them to you and make sure none of them end up on the deck."

Devin, silent, continued staring at her.

Jessie sighed. "Yes." She braced her hands behind her on the kitchen counter. "Mr. Holt has blond hair and is a twin. Like you and Cody."

She waited for what she knew would come next: Devin's piercing questions regarding Holt's identity, and any possible relation to him and Cody. How in the world was she going to answer him?

But Devin, thankfully, didn't pursue it. Instead, he walked across the kitchen, took the plastic bag from her and headed for the back exit of the cabin.

Jessie followed a few steps behind and lingered in the doorway as Devin carefully walked over to where she'd worked previously, sat down and watched Holt explain to Cody and Miles which tools to hand him as he worked to repair joists on the opposite side of the deck.

Devin didn't speak; he simply studied Holt, watching his face, studying his movements, his thoughtful expression deepening as he stared.

"I'll need to put some scaffolding in place before we can start." Holt stood from his kneeling position in front of the boys and propped his hands on his hips. "It'll take a while to get this done, boys. I can definitely use your help, but you sure you want to sacrifice your free time in the afternoons working on this?"

Cody beamed. "Yes!"

Miles looked at Cody and Jessie, then tilted his head back and looked at Holt, saying quietly, "Yes, please."

Slowly, Holt knelt again and held out his hand. "Thank you, Miles," he said. "Offering your help is truly a gentlemanly thing to do."

Miles blushed, his lips tipping up at the corners, and shook Holt's hand. "You're welcome."

A slow smile spread across Jessie's face as Miles drew his shoulders back and lifted his chin, the brief attention from Holt seeming to bolster his confidence. It was amazing, really, how such a small bit of personal attention from this big, impressive man could warm Miles's heart…and her own as well.

She stiffened, her fingertips touching the base of her throat.

"…in town. Jessie?" Holt was facing her now, concern creasing his brow, as the boys pilfered through a toolbox resting on the deck nearby. "Did you hear me? I said I'm going to work on the deck during the day and in the afternoons with the boys, but I was wondering if it's okay if I spend my lunch break in town? And the evenings, too? After the boys and I finish up for the day?"

"O-of course." She forced a smile, trying—and failing—to still the questions popping up in her own mind. "Your free time is your own. You're welcome to do with it what you'd like."

But where would he spend all that time? And with whom?

Chapter Eleven

Two weeks later Holt sat on his backside in dirt, laughing as Cody, Miles and Devin struggled to yank a vine from one of the thick legs of the wooden benches surrounding the fire pit outside Creek Cabin.

"It might help if y'all pulled in the same direction," he said, leaning back onto his hands. "You know, line your hands up on the vine, decide which direction to pull then give it the ol' heave-ho."

Devin, who'd served as the leader on this particular project for the past ten minutes, released the vine and stepped back. "All right," he said, pointing at Miles first, then Cody. "Miles, you take the bottom hold because you're the strongest."

"No, he's not," Cody said. "I'm strong, too."

Devin heaved out a heavy breath. "I'm not

saying you're not strong, Cody. I'm just saying Miles is the strongest out of all of us."

A wide smile appeared on Miles's face and his chest puffed out just a bit with pride, prompting a deeper chuckle from Holt.

Miles assumed the position Devin directed and after Miles had wrapped his small hands around the lowest part of the vine, Cody moved in next, grabbed the vine just above Miles's hands and waited for Devin to join them.

"Now, when I give the signal," Holt said, "I want all of you to yank as hard as you can, okay?"

The trio shouted *yes, sir* almost in unison and once Devin fastened his hands securely around the vine and braced his legs, Holt gave the command.

"Pull!"

In unison, the boys yanked hard on the tightly coiled vine, pulling backward in one direction. It gave way, snapping at the base, unraveled almost instantly from the bench's leg and sprang free, leaving the boys stumbling backward onto their backsides in a heap. Legs and arms entwined, the boys laughed and rolled apart, tears of laughter mixing with dirt as they scrambled to their feet.

Cody, breathing hard, brushed the dirt off his palms, jogged over and grabbed Holt's hand. "That was the last one, Mr. Holt. Come try out the bench with me."

Holt shoved to his feet and let Cody lead him over to the bench, then sat on the smooth wooden seat.

Cody plopped down beside him and dragged the back of his hand across his sweaty forehead. "Whew! That was the toughest one, Mr. Holt."

He laughed again. It had been. For the past two hours, he and the boys had spent their Saturday morning clearing deadfall and dead leaves—the last of winter's debris—from the small clearing beside Creek Cabin. They'd tackled the wooden benches next, unwinding, twisting and pulling tangled clumps of vines from all three benches, and clearing broken tree limbs from the fire circle itself, exposing a large span of dirt circled by large stones of various colors.

The boys had worked hard during what should've been their free time this morning just as they had every afternoon after school for the past two weeks. With their help, he and Jessie had managed to replace all of the rotten deck boards on Creek Cabin's back deck and give it a beautiful dark stain. They'd also swept off the porch and cleaned the accompanying Adirondack chairs as well as spruced up the landscaping by trimming the hedges surrounding the cabin and planting tiny blue petunia plants along the front porch. And now the fire pit was ready, save for wiping the winter mold and grime from the benches.

"They were all tough." Devin stood, held out a hand and helped Miles to his feet. "We might not have gotten that one loose if Miles hadn't helped us."

Miles, grinning, skipped over to the bench and sat on the other side of Cody. "Wouldn't none of us got it down without Mr. Holt."

"Thank you, Miles," Holt said. "You're turning out to be a true gentleman in every way."

And it was true. As they'd worked over the past couple of weeks, Miles had gained a bit more confidence each day, every task lifting his head a bit more and putting a proud look in his eyes. He'd grown more comfortable in Holt's presence, asking to help with each task almost as eagerly as Cody.

"And me, too?" Cody asked. "I'm turning out to be a gentleman, too, ain't I?"

Holt smiled wide and ruffled Cody's hair, saying softly, "Yes, you are. You're a gentleman in every way."

And he couldn't be prouder. Cody and Devin, both, had not only worked hard and followed direction well but had grown as com-

fortable with him as Miles had—Cody even
more so.

It felt so good to have his sons in his life
again, though… Holt's smile slipped. He
wished it were on a permanent basis and that
Cody and Devin knew who he really was and
what he wanted to be to them. He couldn't
imagine how wonderful it'd feel to hear them
call him Dad. Right now, even the thought itself felt foreign, but with hard work, dedication
and careful consideration of everyone's feelings, he truly thought it could become a reality. And despite his best efforts to the contrary,
he couldn't help but feel resentful of having to
keep his identity secret.

Two small hands nudged his knees apart as
Devin pushed his way in between Holt's legs
and leaned close to his face.

Holt stilled as Devin's eyes, the same shade
of hazel as his own, perused his face. "What
is it, Devin?"

Devin's gaze returned to Holt's then strayed
again, moving in tandem with his hand to
Holt's hair where it stilled. "Can I?"

Unsure what he wanted but equally unwill-
ing to refuse any request as Devin rarely made
them, Holt nodded.

Devin slowly sifted his fingers through the
strands of Holt's hair. Devin's hand lowered,

his fingertips tracing Holt's brow, straight nose then chin, his thumb and forefinger settling on either side of his jaw. His hand settled there, Devin's gaze moving slowly between Holt's face and Cody's as they sat beside each other on the bench, his nails lightly scratching the stubble lining Holt's jaw as he stared.

Holt's mouth parted on a small breath. Ever since their conversation about him having a twin brother, Devin had been especially observant, watching his every move, scrutinizing his features and examining Cody's compared to his. Devin was smart, just as Jessie had said, and Holt was worried Devin had picked up more than he and Jessie gave the boy credit for.

"What is it, Devin?" he asked softly.

Fingers stilling, Devin met Holt's eyes again then backed away from him, frowning.

"I see y'all managed to conquer that monster vine." Twigs snapped underfoot as Jessie strolled across the clearing and joined them at the fire pit. She held a pack of scrubbing sponges in one hand and a bucket of soapy water in the other. "I brought some supplies to clean the benches with and once we take care of that, I think we can knock off for the day."

She halted abruptly by the fire pit, glancing between Holt and Devin.

"Everything okay?" she asked.

Breaking eye contact with Devin, Holt stood and nodded. "I can't take credit for the monster vine." He managed to smile as Devin walked around the fire pit and sat on the opposite bench, apparently deep in thought. "The boys took care of that on their own."

"Miles was the strongest," Cody finally admitted, springing off the bench and grabbing Holt's hand. "Wasn't he, Mr. Holt?"

Holt squeezed Cody's hand in his, the act having become familiar—automatic, even—over their days spent together. "Yeah, I'd say so, though all of you are plenty strong."

"But not as strong as you." Cody bounced in place with excitement, shaking Holt's hand up and down. "You can lift the big deck boards by yourself, ride the bulls and wrestle—"

"All right, already." Jessie laughed. "We all know how strong Mr. Holt is. Goodness knows he sure has spruced up Creek Cabin in record time."

The compliment warmed Holt's cheeks—and heart. Throughout their time together over the past couple of weeks, Jessie had slowly begun giving him the lead more and more when it came to the renovation tasks. As soon as the overhaul of Creek Cabin's deck had been completed without a hitch, she'd turned the to-do list completely over to him along with free rein as to what they tackled next each day. And she hadn't sat on the sidelines, either. She'd worked just as hard—if not harder—as he and the boys had, tackling each laborious task with gusto then, once the sun set, returning to her daily tasks for the shelter inside the cabin.

Each night Holt returned from visiting Ava, he'd noticed the lights on in her cabin and sometimes had been able to see her silhouette in the window as he'd driven by, sometimes sweeping or mopping, washing dishes, folding laundry. Once, he'd even spotted her chopping more firewood by Hummingbird Haven's community cabin. She'd looked up when the truck's headlights had flooded over her and waved Holt off when he'd offered to stop and help.

One thing he'd learned for sure about Jessie was that she felt the most comfortable when she was in control. But now, as he studied the dark shadows that had formed under her eyes, he realized that need for control—at least while he was present at Hummingbird Haven—had begun wearing her down. She put everyone before herself and never stopped to pamper herself.

An almost overwhelming urge waved over him to cradle her in his arms, hold her close and protect her. Jessie deserved a break. More than that. She deserved to be catered to, to be considered and cared for in a way that left her feeling valued…treasured even.

"Don't I owe you a dinner?"

Jessie, amid passing scrubbing sponges out to the boys, stopped and glanced at him. "What do you mean?"

Holt smiled. "I mean, you and Zoe have taken over preparing the afternoon snacks for the past couple of weeks and barely let me help."

"That's because you were busy out here," she said. "We didn't want to disturb you when you were making such good progress."

Holt held up a hand. "I know, and it wasn't an accusation, just an observation. Plus, Zoe and the boys cooked a great breakfast for me the first morning I woke up here, and Peggy Ann and her daughters have had to step in and help out with cooking dinners on the nights you've stayed late to help me out here. So I figure the least I—and the boys—could do would be to cook dinner for all of you."

Jessie considered this, tilting her head and smiling. "Hmm. I think that might go over well. What night were you thinking?"

"Oh, I figure it'll take…" Holt glanced around. "Maybe two or three more days to finish getting Creek Cabin spic-and-span, inside as well as out, and I'd need a couple more days to plan the menu and pick up food and decorations. So maybe next Sunday after we all get back from church?"

Jessie made a confused face. "Decorations?"

Holt smiled. "You know it. This will be a celebratory dinner for the completion of Creek Cabin renovations and you, Zoe, Peggy Ann and her daughters will be the guests of honor."

"Oh, I see." She grinned. "I think Zoe would like that." She laughed. "Very much!"

"What're you going to cook?" Cody asked, tugging Holt's hand again.

Holt raised a brow. "Don't you mean what're we going to cook?"

"Is this another gentleman lesson?" Cody asked.

"Yep." Holt propped his fists on his hips and thrust his chest out. "Every gentleman should know his way around a grill." He eyed Jessie as she laughed louder. "Is there a grill at Hummingbird Haven?"

Jessie's laughter trailed away and she wiped her eyes, smiling. "We have one, though I wasn't aware operating a grill was meant solely for men."

Holt dipped his head, producing a sly smile. "Forgive me. I meant operating the grill will be a job for the gentlemen during this celebration. All the ladies will be expected to do is sit back, relax, enjoy a good meal and let the gentlemen cater to them. I promise you you'll enjoy every moment."

Jessie smiled, her gaze lowering to his smile. Her cheeks flushed a pretty pink then darkened almost the same shade as her auburn hair before she shook her head and resumed passing out the scrubbing sponges to the boys. "If you say so."

Holt smiled wider. Her words didn't offer much encouragement, but that pretty blush did.

Jessie hadn't been sure what to expect at Holt's celebratory dinner but surprisingly, she was enjoying herself.

"Now, I know Katie and Tabitha want their hamburgers with extra cheese," Holt said as he stood at the grill on the back deck of Creek Cabin, "but how would you like your steak cooked, Peggy Ann?"

Peggy Ann, seated on one side of a large folding table set with a bright pink tablecloth and pink paper plates, smiled. "Medium-well, please."

Holt lifted the spatula he held in the air. "Medium-well it is, then. Gentlemen, since the food's about ready, would you please offer the ladies a beverage?"

Cody, Miles and Devin, all clad in baggy aprons and oversize chef hats, marched across the deck, carrying pitchers of soda, tea or water, and stood in front of the table.

"What would you pur-fur, ma'am?" Cody asked, tilting up his chin and beaming.

Katie and Tabitha, seated on either side of Peggy Ann, covered their smiles and giggled, before they each burst out with an answer: "Soda!"

"Tea!"

Jessie grinned. Holt and the boys had worked hard putting this dinner together and it showed. The pink tablecloth and chef uniforms were the tip of the iceberg. Glass vases shined in the Sunday afternoon sunlight and bright pink-and-white rhododendron blooms spilled elegantly over the rims and trailed onto the table. Pink plastic cups, pink paper plates and white plastic silverware comprised the place settings and—though this was a touch of God's hand rather than Holt's—a chorus of birdsong drifted across the creek below them on a warm spring breeze.

It was a perfect afternoon for an outdoor celebratory dinner and more fun than Jessie had expected.

"Jessie." Holt's tone held a hint of warning. A lock of blond hair escaped his chef's cap and flopped endearingly over his forehead as he waved his spatula toward the table. "You're not sitting down and relaxing."

Jessie laughed then saluted. "Yes, sir."

She walked over to the table and sat beside Zoe, opposite Peggy Ann and her daughters.

Zoe elbowed her side. "Can you believe this? Chef's hats and all?" She whistled low. "Mercy. He's pulled out all the stops. Only thing missing is candlelight." She grinned. "He gave that a try, too, from what Cody told me when we arrived. Said Holt lit two candles several times but the wind kept blowing them out."

Jessie cast a subtle glance at Peggy Ann as she chatted on the other side of the table with her daughters and smiled. "It's a nice gesture," she whispered in Zoe's ear. "Peggy Ann's been working a lot of hours lately and she and the girls haven't had an afternoon together like this in ages."

Zoe leaned closer, her whisper tickling Jessie's ear. "I don't think Holt did all of this solely for Peggy Ann's benefit."

Jessie batted Zoe's teasing face away and rolled her eyes. "For the boys, then. Holt knew they deserved a special day."

"And you," Zoe murmured, lifting her napkin and spreading it across her lap. "He knew you deserved a break, too."

Her cheeks heating, Jessie waved her hand in front of her face as though batting away a pesky gnat, hoping the extra breeze would cool her overheated skin and hide her expression. Deep down, she knew this day had been for Peggy Ann and the kids, but it was tempting to think that Holt might have thought of her as well. That maybe, just maybe, she crossed his mind once in a while because she still thought of him—much more than she expected and definitely much more than she'd like to admit.

Every day at lunchtime and every night when the day's work was done, she'd watch him climb into his truck, crank the engine and drive off without a word as to where he was going or what he was doing. She'd sit at the window and watch as he returned over an hour later each time, watching as he drove slowly up the driveway, completely disappointed in herself for the prickle of irrational jealousy as to where he was spending his time—or more to the point, with whom.

She'd seen firsthand over the past few weeks how much of a gentleman he was, but like his friend Ty had said, *Old habits die hard.* How many of Holt's old habits had he actually left behind?

Somehow, over the past few weeks, the attraction she'd felt for Holt had begun blossoming into something more. Every gallant gesture, kind word and tender demeanor he displayed touched her heart more and more, deepening her feelings for him. She'd finally begun to admit—at least to herself—that she wanted to believe he'd fully reformed, not just for Cody and Devin's sakes, but for her own.

"Dinner is served," Holt's deep voice boomed proudly.

Two hours later all but one quarter of a hamburger had been eaten, every drop of soda, tea and water had been consumed and the sun hung low in the late-afternoon sky.

Cody, seated beside Zoe at the table, slumped back in his chair and rubbed his belly as he groaned. "I stuffed my gut."

Devin, eyes heavy and seated beside Cody, lowered his chin onto his folded arms. "Me, too." A yawn overtook him. "And I'm kinda tired."

Zoe wiped her mouth and tossed her napkin on the table. "I think it's time little boys took a bath and got in bed."

Cody and Devin sprang upright in their chairs and shouted, "Nuh-uh!"

Zoe laughed. "Yeah-huh!" She stood, pushed her chair in and squeezed each boy's shoulders. Miles was last and she kissed the top of his head, making him giggle. "Come on, you three. How 'bout you come back to my cabin and once y'all have had your baths, we'll watch a movie until it's time for bed?"

Jessie stood, too, and smiled. "You sure you want to take that on, Zoe? Even tired, my boys can—" She clamped her mouth shut and glanced at Holt, the sadness moving through his expression making her cringe. Oh, boy. The last thing she wanted to do was offend him—especially after he'd gone to so much trouble to be kind. "Cody and Devin can be a handful even when they're run-down," she amended, offering a tentative smile.

Holt dipped his head but didn't smile as he watched the boys take off their chef's hats and aprons, then gather their paper plates, plastic cups and silverware and toss them in the trash can Holt had set out earlier.

"I don't mind." Zoe grinned. "Besides, Miles and I like having company, don't we, dude?"

Miles nodded and hugged Zoe's waist as Cody and Devin hustled over and hugged Jessie.

"Don't forget to wash behind your ears." Jessie tugged their earlobes and kissed their cheeks. "And don't give Zoe a hard time, okay? I'll be by to get you when it gets close to bed-time."

"Yes, ma'am." Cody kissed her back then slipped out of her arms, jogged over to Holt and threw himself against Holt's middle. "You wanna come watch a movie with us, Mr. Holt?"

Holt glanced at his watch and grimaced. "I'd love to, but I have somewhere to be tonight. Maybe another time?"

Jessie stiffened, wondering for the umpteenth time where he went when he left every day.

"Sure thing." Cody looked up, his arms around Holt's waist and chin resting against Holt's flat abs. "Thanks for the party. I had a great time."

Holt's smile returned as he looked down at Cody and ruffled his blond hair, a fond act Jessie had noticed Holt do often. She looked away, the sight of Cody hugging Holt with innocent abandon flooding her with bittersweet emotion.

Devin walked hesitantly toward Holt and smiled up at him but didn't offer a hug. Instead, he waved. "It was fun, Mr. Holt. Thank you."

Holt's smile faded. "You're welcome, Devin."

"We had a wonderful time as well," Peggy Ann said, leaving her seat and motioning for her daughters to follow. "Thank you for the dinner, Holt. It's been ages since the girls and I shared an afternoon like this together and we've never had a man cook for—" Blinking rapidly, she waved a hand in the air and smiled. "This was so considerate of you and just what we needed."

Jessie watched, surprised, as Peggy Ann offered her hand to Holt.

He accepted the handshake, returning it gently and said softly, "It was a pleasure, Peggy Ann, and if ever you and the girls need anything, please don't hesitate. I'm hoping we can be friends."

Peggy Ann nodded. "Me, too."

Visions blurring with tears of her own, Jessie turned away and started stacking dirty plates and cups and tossing them into the trash. Moments later Peggy Ann and the girls left, their footsteps and happy chatter fading away.

"Jessie?"

Her hands stilled in the middle of folding the pink tablecloth and she faced Holt again. He stood in the same spot, a somber look in his eyes.

"I think Devin is beginning to realize who I am."

She blew out a heavy breath and sank back against the table. "I guessed that was coming. Ever since you told him you were a twin, he's been thinking and wondering. But—"

"But what?" Holt moved closer, the expression on his face more intense. "Don't you think it's time we tell them? Has anything I've done—anything at all—over the past several weeks helped you see that I'm a different man than I was?"

She closed her eyes, the pain in his voice sending a wave of guilt through her. "Yes. Everything you've done has been considerate and magnanimous and kind but—"

"Then no more *buts*." He shook his head. "Devin will realize it soon enough. Last weekend when we were cleaning the fire pit, he looked at me strangely. Touched my face and seemed to be comparing my features to Cody's. He's a smart boy—"

"I know." Jessie opened her eyes, wanting to give in, wanting to comply with his request and follow through with what she'd hoped might not occur. "I just can't bring myself to shatter Cody and Devin's trust in you. You're getting along so well with them that it may break their hearts to know that—that you…"

"Abandoned them?"

Her chin trembled. She rolled her lips together tightly and tried to steel herself against an onslaught of pain.

"I'm not that man anymore. I'm not the same man you met seven years ago."

She wanted to believe him. She wanted to believe so badly but—

"You're never going to truly trust me, are you?" Holt moved closer. His warm knuckles touched her chin, tilting her face up to his. "No matter what I do, you'll never trust the man I am now because of the man I once was."

The gentle touch of his hand beneath her chin and the pleading look in his eyes coaxed tears to her eyes. She blinked up at him, struggling to speak, but her throat was so tight with emotion, she could only open and close her mouth silently.

He stared down at her a moment more, then his touch left her skin and he walked away, each of his long strides widening the distance between them.

Half an hour later Jessie stood in the hallway of Hope Springs Hospital, staring into Ava's nursery, her heartbeat pounding in her ears.

"This is who you've been seeing during your lunch break and evenings?" Jessie whispered, a flutter of affection stealing her breath.

Holt stood by Ava's crib, Ava cradled snugly in his brawny arms, her wide eyes blinking up at him, her mouth curved in a smile as she babbled happily. Surprised, he looked at Jessie, studied her expression for a moment then frowned. "Who did you think I was seeing?"

Heat scorched her face, from the hairline on her forehead all the way down the back of her neck. Oh, gosh. She'd never felt more embarrassed—or nosy—in her life, but earlier, after watching Holt walk away, she hadn't been able to quell her curiosity…or that nagging bit of jealousy that wouldn't let her rest. So she'd followed him and now she felt like a complete idiot.

"I…well, I just thought—"

"You thought things that may have been true seven years ago, but wouldn't be true now," he said quietly. A small grin curved his lips despite the wounded look in his eyes. "Though I have to say, I'm flattered you cared enough to check up on me." He tilted his head toward the rocking chair beside the crib. "Please, have a seat."

She bit her lip but did as he asked, then folded her hands together in her lap. Her fingers shook and she squeezed them together to still their nervous tremble.

"Here." Holt moved closer, bent and placed Ava in her arms. "Talk to her. She loves a good conversation in the evening."

Jessie cradled Ava in her arms and smiled down at her through a sheen of tears. "Hello, beautiful," she whispered.

Ava stared up at her, eyes wide, still smiling around another bout of babbles.

"I've been thinking about her a lot since we first came here," Holt said, kneeling on one knee beside her. He cupped Ava's downy head, his big thumb smoothing gently across her soft cheek. "I couldn't help thinking about her alone here, in her crib, without someone holding her, telling her they cared about her."

Jessie sniffed, her throat tightening to the point of pain. "Holt…"

"I understand," he whispered. His hand left Ava and lifted to Jessie's cheek instead, his big palm settling against her skin, his thumb brushing over her trembling mouth. "It's hard for me to accept, but I understand why you have trouble trusting me."

She blinked hard but a lone tear escaped, falling from her lower lashes and settling in the corner of her mouth.

His thumb touched the corner of her mouth, moving the tear to his fingertip. "I never knew how hard it must've been for you accepting Cody and Devin that night seven years ago. How many painful memories I brought to your door with my actions, and how much you must've resented me for it."

She slid one hand out from under Ava and took his hand in hers, squeezing. "I don't re-sent you being here and I'm no longer afraid of letting you in anymore. I just need more time before we tell them."

"How much time?"

"I don't know," she whispered. "And I don't know how to explain. It's just that… I'm still worried."

Pain flickered through Holt's expression. "About what?"

About the future. About her feelings for him, which grew stronger every day.

Over the past month Holt had slipped beneath her defenses as easily as he had Cody and Devin's. In the beginning, she'd expected Holt to fumble through her to-do list and falter in reconnecting with his sons. Instead, he'd met every challenge she'd thrown his way, exceeded her expectations by going out of his way to be respectful of Peggy Ann and her girls and had shown genuine affection and dedication for Cody and Devin. And he had been just as considerate of her own concerns and wishes.

Holt had proven himself to be a good man who deserved an opportunity to become the devoted father his sons deserved.

But Zoe had been right on day one. There was no way to move forward without someone's heart breaking. And what worried Jessie the most was that she knew she would never be able to bring herself to break Holt's. Which meant her future with Cody and Devin would no longer be the same as she'd once pictured it.

"I'm worried about what comes next," she whispered.

He shook his head slowly, confusion in his eyes as he leaned closer. "You have nothing to worry about. Whatever happens, I've told you that you'll always be Cody and Devin's mother. We'll work this out. We're in this together."

Oh, how she wanted that. More than he knew.

"I'd like to take my sons home," he said softly. "Just for a visit so my mother and brother can meet them. And I'd like you to come with us, so I can show you what I have to offer them. To prove to you that I mean to be the best father possible. We don't have to tell them who I am yet. It'll just be a little trip— a vacation of sorts—when the boys are out of school. Will you let me do that, Jessie? I promise I won't let you down."

She brought his palm to her mouth and kissed the center of it softly, watching his eyes darken as her lips touched his skin.

"Okay," she whispered. "I trust you."

Chapter Twelve

Three weeks later Jessie peered out the passenger window of Holt's truck, barely able to take her eyes off the sprawling green landscape lined with white fencing. The sun's afternoon rays poured golden warmth across acres of lush grass, colorful wildflowers and blooming southern magnolia trees, their bountiful creamy blooms along the white fence lending an elegant air to the grounds.

"Are we there yet?" Cody piped for the trillionth time from the backseat of the cab.

Holt, seated in the driver's seat, chuckled. "Yes, we're here." His smile widened as he navigated the truck up a long, winding paved drive toward a white, two-story house with a wraparound porch and immaculate landscaping. "Finally."

Holt's voice held a heavy dose of dispelled impatience, which Jessie understood.

After their visit to the Boarder Baby Unit three weeks ago, she and Holt had decided to take the boys to Pine Creek Farm over spring break. Until then, he'd continued working his way through the to-do list she'd given him, had added a few tasks of his own and had kept to his usual schedule of working at the shelter during the school day, spending every afternoon with Cody, Devin and Miles, and visiting Ava during his lunch and in the evening. Up to this point, the only change in routine had been that Jessie began accompanying Holt on his visits to Ava and they'd taken turns feeding her, changing her diaper and making her laugh.

Well, that hadn't been the only change.

Jessie glanced at Holt under her lashes, noting the excitement in his expression. The time she'd spent with Ava had not only strengthened her bond with the baby but also with Holt. She'd grown comfortable riding in the passenger seat of his truck, sharing funny anecdotes about the boys when they were little, catching Holt up on all their likes and dislikes and academic mishaps and successes thus far. And, in the midst of it all, they'd found themselves laughing at each other's jokes, sharing a Big Mouth cup of soda they'd pick up from a local gas station after a long day of work on the way to see Ava. And every evening, before Holt retired to Creek Cabin for the night, he took her to the door of her cabin, hugged the boys goodnight and stood outside on the front porch until he heard the lock on the door click shut. Then he'd climb back into his truck and drive off to his cabin alone.

More often than not, Jessie would walk from window to window in her cabin, watching the red taillights of his truck until they faded out of view among the dark trees.

She'd fallen for him. She could admit it now—at least to herself—which complicated matters all the more.

Now they'd finally arrived at Holt's family farm and from the look on Holt's face, it was clear this introduction—despite not revealing the full truth to Cody and Devin—would be a massive step forward in Holt's mind.

"Ah, there's my mom," Holt said. "Sitting on the porch already."

Jessie tore her gaze from the lush rolling green hills of the pasture and focused on the older woman sitting in a rocking chair on the porch. She sprang to her feet as soon as she noticed the truck and ran down the steps to the driveway, calling to someone over her shoulder as she went.

"That's your mom?" Devin echoed, craning his neck for a better view. "What's her name?"

"Gayle." Holt smiled and glanced in the rearview mirror at Devin, before parking the truck. "I mean, Mrs. Gayle."

He exited the truck, opened the back door of the cab and started helping the boys out of the backseat.

"You're home!" Holt's mom, a lovely woman with long gray hair, met Holt at the front of the truck and enveloped him in a big bear hug. "Oh, how I've missed you. Every day seemed like a month!"

Holt hugged her back and kissed her cheek, the tenderness in his expression unmistakable.

A wistful smile lifted Jessie's mouth. What did that feel like? Coming home to a biological parent you knew? One who raised you from birth and loved you—unconditionally in most cases? And how would it feel to have a home to return to? A place where your most cherished memories resided around every corner? A place that resided in your heart no matter where you traveled, where those who loved you waited eagerly for you to return?

She'd wondered often over the years. Each time she'd helped place a child in a loving adoptive home, she'd looked on as a child she'd loved was united with a new family in a new home and wondered what that child's life would look like years from then. How that child would feel years down the road as an adult, coming home from their travels, embracing their new parents.

Holt, smiling, eased out of his mother's embrace, bent his head and kissed her cheek again. "I missed you, too, Mom."

Jessie's smile faded. It'd feel just like that, she supposed. Like the reverent tenderness in Holt's relieved smile and the admiring adoration in Gayle's loving gaze. Togetherness, support and protection. Strength in numbers. Something Cody and Devin would benefit strongly from.

"So you're Holt's mom." Cody had strolled around to the front of the truck, stood beside Holt and shaded his eyes from the strong afternoon sun.

Gayle, an eager light in her eyes, lifted her arms and stepped forward then stopped abruptly. She glanced at Holt, who shook his head, then lowered her arms and refocused on Cody. Her chin trembled.

"Yes," she said, her tone gentle. "I'm Mrs. Gayle and I'm so glad you've come to visit." She held out her hand. "May I shake your hand, please?"

Cody grinned. "Sure." He slid his small palm into hers and she immediately covered their entwined hands with her free one as though cradling his palm. "A gentleman always shakes hands when they meet a new person." He glanced up at Holt. "That's lesson number seven, right?"

"Eight." Devin, his hands shoved deep in his pockets, strolled to the front of the truck and stood beside Cody.

Gayle, her chin still trembling, slowly released Cody's hand and reached for Devin's. "You must be Devin. I'm so glad to finally meet you."

Devin hesitated, turned his head and rose up on his toes, his eyes meeting Jessie's where she still sat in the passenger seat of the truck. There was a question in his gaze, a silent request for permission.

Smiling, Jessie nodded.

Devin faced Gayle again, removed his hand from his pocket and shook her hand. "It's nice to meet you, Mrs. Gayle."

The passenger door of the truck opened and Jessie, startled, looked up as a man, identical to Holt, looked back at her, one of his muscular arms propped on the open door of the truck and the other hanging freely by his side.

"You gonna join us?" A polite smile crossed his lips, but his eyes remained guarded. "We won't bite, I promise."

Liam, Jessie presumed. She dipped her head

in acknowledgment and got out of the truck, briefly accepting the helping hand he offered as she lowered her feet to the paved driveway.

"I'm L—"

"Liam. Holt's brother." Jessie studied his features. "You look exactly alike."

He grinned. "He's fortunate to have my looks."

Holt raised an eyebrow. "Your looks? You took after me."

Liam laughed harder then embraced Holt, slapping his back heartily before releasing him. "Good to have you back, brother."

Holt tipped his chin. "You missed me that much?"

"At five in the morning when it's time to muck the stalls?" Liam nodded. "Oh, yeah. And by the way, now that you're back, that'll be your job starting tomorrow, seeing as how I've lined up a trail ride for you and your guests." He spun around, eyed Cody and Devin, who stared at him with curious eyes, then lowered to his haunches, bringing his eyes to the level of theirs. "How 'bout that, boys?" His tone softened as he studied their faces. "You two interested in riding a horse tomorrow and seeing the lay of the land around these parts?"

Devin nodded slowly, seemingly almost mesmerized by Liam's presence. He moved close to Liam, staring up at his face, and smiled. "You're Mr. Holt's brother."

"Yeah," he said. "I'm Liam." He lifted his hand toward Devin then stilled, asking softly, "Mind if I take a look at you?"

Devin shook his head and lifted his chin, almost in invitation.

Smile widening, Liam brushed Devin's blond bangs back with gentle fingers then held his chin between his thumb and forefinger, turning Devin's head one way then the other.

"Yeah." Liam's tone was thick with emotion, and he seemed to catch himself, releasing Devin's chin and easing back on his haunches. "You'll do, kid." He stood and cleared his throat. "You stash your bags in the back, Holt?" At his nod, he sauntered toward the back of the truck. "I'll start moving those in."

Devin followed Liam, his steps falling inches behind the older man's. "Can I help, Mr. Liam?"

Liam stopped. "Well, let's see." He reached out and squeezed Devin's upper arms. "Those are impressive muscles you got there. I can definitely use your help."

"And mine, too?" Cody asked, jogging over to join Liam and Devin.

Liam grinned and tapped Cody's chin with his knuckle. "I'd love your help. Now, let's get to hauling."

"Jessie."

Pulling her attention away from the boys' excited faces, she turned and found Gayle standing beside her, tears brimming along her lower lashes. She wrapped her arms around Jessie, embracing her closely.

"Thank you for letting Holt bring them home," Gayle said, her words a soft whisper against Jessie's ear. "I can't tell you how much this means to all of us." She pulled back and tucked a strand of hair behind Jessie's ear, her voice shaking with emotion as she met Jessie's eyes. "And thank you so much for being there for Cody and Devin. From what Holt has told us, the boys couldn't have had a better mother."

Gayle hugged her again, holding her so tight, Jessie could feel her heartbeat against her chest.

Eyes burning, Jessie sank into the embrace, a sweet tenderness enveloping her entire being, all the way to the tips of her toes.

"Okay, Mom." Holt's voice sounded near Jessie's ear as he tugged Gayle's arms away from Jessie. "Let's not smother her right off the bat, all right?"

Gayle laughed and wiped tears from her cheeks as she hugged Holt again. "I'm just so happy to have you back. And the boys…" Her voice caught. "It's like a dream come true."

She released Holt and shook her head. "Y'all must be famished after the long ride here." She hustled off, heading for the front steps as she said over her shoulder, "Come on in! I've got dinner hot and ready. There's fried chicken, mashed potatoes, sweet potatoes, green beans seasoned with ham hock, broccoli casserole, baked mac and cheese, apple pie, corn on the cob..."

Holt blew out a breath as Gayle entered the house still rattling off the list of Southern delicacies she'd prepared. "Hope you're hungry." He looked down at Jessie. "The way Mom cooks there's probably enough in there to feed fifty people and send 'em home with two days' worth of leftovers." He held out his hand. "Shall we?"

The boyish grin on his face sent a delicious thrill of excitement through her. Strangely, feeling years younger—as though the future stretched far ahead, brighter than ever—she slid her hand into his and nodded.

Dinner turned out to be exactly all that Holt predicted and Jessie had enjoyed every moment.

Gayle had covered every inch of the large dining room table on the first floor of the main house with beautiful dishes stuffed to the brim with mouthwatering casseroles, seasoned vegetables, dinner rolls and desserts of every kind. The tantalizing aroma filled the entire first floor of the house and filled the senses as fully as the food did their hungry bellies.

"Gracious, Mom." Holt, seated between Jessie and Cody, eased back in his chair and rubbed his flat midsection. "That was delicious, but I think I gained ten pounds in one meal."

Liam chuckled. "Get used to it. She's been cooking all week—ever since you called to say you were coming home—so you'll be eating like this at every meal."

"I hope I made enough for the whole week." Gayle, seated opposite Jessie, leaned across the table and patted Holt's hand. "Y'all are staying for the entire week, right? That's what you said on the phone?"

Holt nodded. "Cody and Devin are out of school this entire week for spring break."

Gayle's expression brightened. "Then maybe you can stay a bit longer? Over the weekend, too?"

Jessie looked down, removed her napkin from her lap, folded it neatly, then placed it on the table beside her plate.

"Mom." Holt's low voice held a note of caution. "Let's not get ahead of ourselves, okay?"

He pushed his chair back, stood and glanced out the wide picture window framing the front lawn. "Dusk is settling. It's 'bout time to go round up the horses and get 'em settled for the night." He smiled at Cody and Devin, who had grown heavy-eyed as they lounged in their seats with full bellies. "But first, I think it's time we take these two upstairs and get 'em ready for bed. Whatcha think, Jessie?"

Heart warming at the sight of the boys' sleepy—but happy—faces, she stood, too. "I think that's a good idea."

The boys grumbled as Holt and Jessie led them upstairs but were too tired from the long day of travel and a good meal to put up much resistance.

"Here's where you guys will sleep," Holt said, opening a door to the left of the stairs on the landing.

Inside, there were two twin beds made up neatly with blue sheets and a white lightweight quilt. A nightstand sat between the beds and long white curtains graced ceiling-to-floor windows on the wall facing the front yard. Liam had placed the boys' overnight bags on the ends of the beds.

Holt pointed at the windows. "Good thing about this room is Jessie won't have to set an alarm for you. Those curtains are transparent, and the sun'll pour right there in the morning and tug your eyes open." He smiled. "Good thing, too, because Liam and I are taking y'all on a trail ride."

Cody clapped his hands. "Will we get to ride a horse of our own?"

Holt nodded but held up a hand. "But you'll have to wear a helmet and follow our directions to the letter—and I mean, to the letter. It's always better to be safe than sorry."

Devin smiled. "Another lesson."

"Yeah." Holt kneeled on the soft beige carpet and spread open his arms. "Can I have a hug before I head out to round up the horses? I won't be back until you're in bed and won't see you again 'til morning."

Cody dashed across the room and threw himself into Holt's arms, hugging his neck and kissing his cheek. Devin moved more slowly but complied, walking over, hugging Holt briefly and murmuring, "Good night, Mr. Holt."

Holt's exuberant expression fell slightly but he smiled and stood, his tone warm. "Good night, Devin. Sleep well."

"Boys, please get your pajamas and toothbrushes out of your bags," Jessie said as she and Holt eased out onto the landing. "I'll be back in a few minutes to help you start your baths." She shut the door behind her and looked expectantly at Holt. "Which room should I stay in?"

Holt led her across the landing to a room opposite the boys'. "Here," he said, nudging open the door.

A queen bed sat center stage, decorated with fluffy pillows and a brightly colored hand-woven quilt. It was positioned opposite the same type of ceiling-to-floor windows as those in the boys' room, offering an unimpeded view of the exquisite grounds below.

Everything she'd seen at Pine Creek Farm so far was elegant and refined but, at the same time, warm and welcoming. Exactly what she'd always imagined a beautiful home should be and the guest quarters, located near the main house, that Gayle rented to overnight visitors, lent an even more picturesque appeal to the grounds.

The thought of Cody and Devin here on a permanent basis, waking up to such splendor, under a roof with so much love, care and attention from a father, grandmother and uncle… well, it made her lone presence and small cabin at Hummingbird Haven pale in comparison.

"This is beautiful, Holt," she said, struggling to smile as she blinked back tears. "Thank you."

Holt's fingertip touched her chin and tilted up her face. His eyes peered down at her, roving over her expression, and his thumb traced the slight wobble in her lower lip.

"Jessie…" His chest rose on a deep inhale, and he moved closer, his palms cupping her cheeks. His expression changed, the happy light in his eyes deepening into warm affection. "I—"

He bit his lip and halted his words, his gaze straying to her mouth.

Jessie studied his expression, her eyes tracing the handsome curves of his face, her face tilting up as though in invitation.

"I'm grateful we met when we did and not before," he whispered. "Because the man I was then wouldn't have treated you the way you deserve." He hesitated, then bent his head, his lips barely brushing her cheek as he whispered, "Good night, Jessie," then turned and walked away.

Jessie went inside the room, shut the door and leaned back against it. She stood that way for several minutes, her palm pressed against her cheek, covering the fading warmth his lips had left behind.

What would it be like to be loved by Holt? To be by his side, treasured, supported and protected? To be welcomed by his family with

open arms as more than just an acquaintance…
but as a part of Holt's family instead?

She closed her eyes and envisioned it, allowing herself to cherish the brief glimpse of a life she'd always imagined but feared would always be out of reach. A life she found herself longing for more than ever. One that included Holt appreciating her as more than just a good person. A life in which Holt admired her as a woman…and loved her as well.

Chapter Thirteen

Something was missing.

"We've got everything, right?" Holt asked, checking his saddlebag one last time. "I feel like we're forgetting something."

Liam, standing nearby, patted his mare's neck and shook his head. "Nope. We planned everything carefully, down to the time it'll take to traverse the trail and back with one break at the creek." He glanced over his shoulder where Jessie and Gayle fussed over Cody and Devin, checking the straps of their riding helmets, making sure they were fully fastened. "No. We're good."

But he wasn't. Holt frowned, taking in his surroundings. The grounds of Pine Creek Farm looked exactly the same as they always had—lush green hills and valleys, clean white fences, immaculate stables, well-maintained guest quarters and a beautiful main house. But something felt off—he rubbed his chest, his blood pulsing beneath his palm—in here. Right where his heart should be.

He'd felt it the moment he'd driven his truck up the long driveway yesterday afternoon. His childhood home looked as welcoming as always and his mom—even Liam, in his own way—had been overjoyed to see him and the boys. Gayle's home cooking had tasted just as delectable as always last night, and the horses had returned under his and Liam's leads to the stables last night peacefully, settling in their cozy stalls for the night.

But the bed Holt had slept in for the past few years had seemed less comfortable, and the sounds outside his window less familiar. He'd tossed and turned for the better part of last night, barely sleeping. When he opened his eyes with the first soft rays of morning sunlight, he'd still felt as though he was in unfamiliar surroundings. A place that looked exactly the same on the outside but began to feel oddly alien to him on the inside.

Even now, standing outside the stables on a beautiful spring morning with clear skies and warm breezes, he still felt out of place somehow.

"Something's missing," he said again, wondering if verbalizing the sensation might dispel the unwelcome emotion.

"I told you, nothing's missing." Liam stopped adjusting the saddle on his horse and walked over, concerned. "Are you okay?"

Holt met his eyes, exactly the same shade as his own, the comforting sensation he usually felt when facing his brother not as strong as in the past. "No," he said. "I don't think I am."

Liam frowned and squeezed his upper arm. "Look, if you're not up to a trail ride today, I don't mind taking Jessie and the boys out on my own—"

"No." The word burst from his lips more sharply than he'd intended.

Nodding slowly, Liam stepped back. "All right." He gestured toward the boys and headed toward them. "We best get the boys settled on their horses if we're gonna make it back in time for the lunch Mom's planned."

"Liam?"

He stopped and glanced back.

Holt summoned a smile. "Thanks for arranging the trail ride today. I think the boys will love it."

Liam shrugged. "Not a problem." He grinned. "Those boys are perfect, Holt."

He nodded, his smile fading as Liam walked over to the boys and double-checked their helmets. Cody and Devin were perfect and having them here at his childhood home should feel perfect, too. But it didn't.

"Come on, slow poke," Cody called out, his hands cupped around his mouth. "Mr. Liam said you're slower than a snail in JELL-O."

Holt laughed, grabbed his horse's reins and walked his mare over. "Well, let's see if we can pick up the pace a bit."

Thirty minutes later they were all saddled up, their horses strolling across the peaceful grounds of Pine Creek Farm in single file.

"And to your left here," Liam said from the head of the line as he pointed at an expansive stretch of green grass, "you'll see one of the pastures where we turn the horses out from time to time."

"How many horses do you have in all?" Devin, riding a gray Welsh pony, followed Liam next in line.

"Twenty-two at the moment," Liam answered, smiling over his shoulder at Devin. "And I'm hoping to snag a pretty quarter mare next week."

"But there ain't one prettier than mine," Cody, third in line, piped. He patted the neck of his chestnut Welsh pony. "Peanut's the best horse in the world."

Jessie, riding behind Cody and in front of

Holt, straightened in her saddle. "Cody, please sit up straight and keep both hands on the reins and saddle horn like Mr. Holt and Mr. Liam taught you."

Holt smiled. "Oh, he's all right, Jessie. He listened and practiced well and Peanut's as calm and gentle as they come. Besides, I'm keeping a close eye on him and if we moved any slower we'd be going backward."

Jessie glanced back at him, that auburn hair of hers trailing below her helmet and almost sparkling in the sunlight as she laughed. "I'm rather fond of the slow pace, thank you very much. Any faster and I'm afraid I'd topple off."

"Yeah." Holt grinned. "I hate to say it, but I kinda noticed that."

Her eyes narrowed at him over her shoulder. "Are you trying to say I'm not a natural with horses?"

Holt burst out laughing. "No, ma'am. I wouldn't say that. I'd like to make it back to the house in one piece."

They continued on, Liam leading the horses along a flat trail that circled the property at a slow, relaxed pace. The grounds were tranquil but busy, the first large group of guests having recently arrived for their spring visit. The visitors milled about the serene grounds, taking in the sights as they strolled across the fields or rode horses along the trails, taking advantage of the cool breezes before the heat of summer sizzled in.

Halfway to the end of the trail, they reached a large pond Liam had stocked with fish. Tall willow trees framed the grassy banks of the sparkling pond, creating a picturesque view.

"Break time," Liam called out, slowing the horses to a stop. "We're gonna hop off and let the horses rest here for a while. Boys, stay put and Holt and I will help you down."

Cody and Devin did as Liam directed. As soon as Holt and Liam lowered them to the ground and helped them remove their helmets, Cody was eager to move.

"Can we go check out the pond?" he asked, already straying in that direction.

Holt glanced at Jessie as she stood beside her mare and removed her helmet. Her cheeks had flushed a pretty pink during the ride and the sunlight had coaxed a couple freckles out along the bridge of her nose.

He smiled. "You mind if I take the boys down to the pond for a few minutes?"

She dragged her hand through the shiny length of her hair and blew out a heavy breath. "Not at all, though I'm going to hang back here and rest a bit." She leaned forward, stretching her hamstrings. "My legs feel like they've been wrapped around a barrel."

Holt laughed. "Yep. That sounds about right. We'll be back soon." He motioned toward the pond. "Follow me, boys. I'll show you where Liam and I used to fish when we were your age."

He led the way down the grassy incline, below the low-hanging branches of the weeping willow trees, to the sandy bank of the pond.

"Right here." Holt walked over to a set of large roots that protruded from the ground and stretched deep into the murky depths of the pond water. He smacked his hand on the knotted roots and grinned. "Right here is where Liam and I snagged a couple bass so big they almost yanked us into the water."

Cody's eyes widened. "Really? That big?"

Holt held up his hands and spread them a good two feet beyond the bass's actual length. "Huge, I tell you. Massive."

Devin smirked. "No bass is that big."

Holt grinned. "Is that so?"

Devin shrugged then walked to the edge of the bank and tapped the surface of the water with the toe of his tennis shoe. "What kind of fish you got in here?"

Holt rubbed his chin. "Oh, bass, bluegill,

threadfin shad and catfish. But it's the bass that put up the biggest fight."

Devin considered this as he eyed the rippling water. "Could we go fishing while we're here?"

"Of course," Holt said. "I'd be happy to take you tomorrow morning, if you'd like?"

"Yay!" Cody shouted, thrusting his arms in the air.

Devin's reaction was much more subtle. "Sure." He looked up and an honest-to-goodness smile appeared. "That'd be cool."

Holt shoved his hands into his pockets to keep from hauling Devin close and smothering him in a bear hug, the empty feeling he'd felt all morning fading just a tad. *Progress*, he thought. *Definitely progress.*

Jessie tilted her head back and drained the last drop of water from the plastic bottle she held. "Oh, boy, that's good."

"Want another?" Liam, standing nearby, reached into his saddlebag.

"Yes, please."

He withdrew an unopened bottle of water and handed it to her.

"Thank you." Jessie unscrewed the cap, brought the bottle to her mouth and tilted it back, closing her eyes as the cool water cascaded down her throat. "Whew." She screwed the cap back on. "I needed that."

Liam retrieved another bottle of water and partook of it himself, tilting the plastic bottle in the direction of the pond as he swallowed. "I imagined Holt's showing the boys our fishing hole. They're probably gonna want to fish themselves once they hear a few of his tall tales from us fishing back in the day."

She followed his gaze to where Holt crouched on the ground near a weeping willow tree, plucking another handful of stones from the ground and passing them to the boys. "Holt's a good man." She blushed as she felt Liam's gaze settle on her profile. "I didn't know him seven years ago when he…well, when he left Cody and Devin with me, so I have no idea who he was then."

"Except for your first impression of him."

She stared as Holt laughed at something Cody said. "Yes."

"And what was that?" he asked. "Your first impression?"

Her cheeks heated. "I thought he was a guy who liked to have fun, had too much fun and then walked away from the consequences." She looked up and met Liam's gaze head-on. "But it wasn't easy for him to walk away from

Cody and Devin and I can say with absolute certainty that he never wanted to."

Holding her gaze, Liam nodded slowly. "Do you know why he walked away despite not wanting to?"

She shook her head.

"He knew he needed to change," Liam said quietly. "He'd taken a wrong turn years earlier, landed on the wrong path and forgot who he was. My dad abandoned me and my mom years ago. Holt and I were teenagers at the time. Young, impressionable. Holt chose to go with him. We didn't hear from him for years and we didn't know about the boys. He was too ashamed to tell us and too guilty for leaving us to come home."

He gestured toward the land around them. Green and pristine. "All this." He shook his head. "It was rotting right where it lay. After our dad and Holt left, the place slowly fell apart. Even the air tasted sour when it hit my tongue. That was bitterness," he said softly. "I resented Holt for years after he left. He walked away as though Mom and I meant nothing to him."

He met her eyes again. "But he came back."

"Yes," she whispered, that bittersweet sensation returning, spearing through her chest. "Yes, he did."

"He's worked so hard to turn his life around," Liam said. "He spent years here, rebuilding the guest houses, sprucing up the land and helping me turn this place around. We sweated, bled and laughed together. Worked every day, sunup to sundown. And eventually, I knew I had my brother back. He's the good man you say he is. He's a better man now than any I've ever met in my lifetime. Cody and Devin—they've changed him for good and the only thing he wants in life now is to be a good father to them. To give them what he should have years ago. Security, love and family." His gaze intensified, a pleading look entering his eyes. "Please don't take those boys away from him. Not now. Not after he's worked so hard and changed so much. It would break his heart if he lost his sons again. He'll give them a good life here."

Jessie turned away, the image of Holt and the boys blurring as she stared at them, and whispered, "I know."

Cody, mouth full of foamy toothpaste, spit in the sink then smiled up at Jessie. "They got bluegills, bass, catfish and thread salad."

Devin, having finished brushing his teeth, wiped his mouth with a hand towel. "Thread-fin shad," he said. "That's what Mr. Liam said they're called."

Cody brushed his teeth and waved a hand in the air. "Woo clares? S'long as you clan hook 'em."

Jessie hid a smile and shook her head. "Cody, please don't speak when your mouth is full."

He frowned up at her. "Blut we ain't eatin'."

"Doesn't matter." Jessie grabbed a hand towel and wiped blue foam from his chin. "If your mouth is full, you shouldn't babble around it. Now, rinse your mouth and meet us in your room. It's getting late and you both need your rest."

"'Cuz we're going fishing!" Cody spit in the sink again, grinned then turned on the tap and shoved his face in the flow of water.

Smiling, Jessie sighed and steered Devin out of the bathroom. "Come on, dude. From the look of his toothpaste face, your brother's going to be a while."

They walked across the landing of Pine Creek Farm's main house and into the room Holt had designated as Cody and Devin's for the duration of their visit.

"What time are we going fishing tomorrow?" Devin asked as he hopped into his twin bed.

"Oh, pretty early, I think." Jessie lifted the covers, waiting as Devin scrambled under them, then covered him up to his chin. "Fish wake up at the crack of dawn and start biting early."

At least, that was what she'd heard. She wasn't a big fisherman herself, but she'd enjoyed it the few times she'd been over the years, and she hoped Cody and Devin would enjoy it tomorrow morning. Holt was definitely excited.

After the trail ride earlier that afternoon, Liam had led them back to the main house for lunch—another round of belly-stuffing delicacies Gayle had prepared special just for them. After everyone pitched in to clean the dishes, Holt and Liam had taken the boys outside for a game of football, which had transitioned into a tour of the guest houses, stables and gardens surrounding the main house.

Regardless of how Liam had described Pine Creek Farm as it had been in the past, the property was certainly beautiful now, and Jessie had trailed behind along the tour of the grounds, admiring every new sight and sound, the boys' excited laughter reminding her time and time again how wonderful a home like this could be for them.

"Jessie?"

She sat on the edge of the bed and brushed Devin's blond bangs out of his eyes. The boys' hair was getting shaggy. It'd be time to cut it soon. "Hmm?"

"Will you be mad if I tell you something?"

Jessie smiled but the heavy tone in his voice made her stomach churn. "I'd like to say no but I won't know until you tell me. How about you give it a shot anyway?"

"But…" His fingers toyed with the quilt that lay beneath his chin. "What if it makes you sad?"

Her smile slipped but she recouped, keeping it firmly in place. "I'll tell you something I want you to remember. You can always be honest with me, no matter what, okay?"

He nodded but remained silent, his eyes roving over her expression, then he whispered quietly—so quietly she had to lean down to hear. "Me and Cody like it here."

He'll give them a good life here.

Her breath caught in her throat. The sentiment Liam had voiced was expected, the same as Devin's. She'd noticed the boys reveling in the beautiful countryside and attention of Holt's extended family over the past days just as she had but facing the thought head-on— the realization that Holt had so much more to offer them than she did—broke her heart all the same.

Maintaining her smile, she covered his hands with hers and struggled to keep the sadness out of her voice. "I'm glad to hear that."

"We like Mr. Holt, Mr. Liam and Mrs. Gayle," he said quietly. "We like the beds, and the horses and the food."

"I think you should tell Mrs. Gayle that. It would warm her heart to know you and Cody love her cooking."

"Could me and Cody come back here again?" he asked.

Her lungs stilled painfully. "I think we could arrange that."

"How long could we stay?"

She hesitated, her throat tightening. "How long would you want to stay?"

He looked down at their hands, his brow creasing, but didn't answer. "Is this what it's like for the others? The ones who get adopted and leave Hummingbird Haven? Do they go to places like this? Places that have a dad, a grandma and an uncle?"

"Yes," she whispered, her heart breaking just a bit more. "Some of them do."

Avoiding her eyes, he asked softly, "Can I ask you one more question?"

"Ask away."

"Who is Mr. Holt?"

Jessie froze, knowing the moment was inevitable given Devin's intellect and curiosity but not ready for what would surely follow once he knew the truth. "What do you mean?"

His eyes returned to hers, a shrewdness that always surprised her shining brightly in his gaze. "Is Mr. Holt my real dad?"

Her mouth opened then closed as she searched for the right words—any words that might help explain their current circumstances. But really, there was only one word that needed to be said. She just wasn't the right person to say it.

Jessie leaned down and kissed Devin's forehead, committing the soft scent of his hair and feel of his small hands between hers to memory, holding on to each moment she had with him and wondering how many she might lose with him and Cody in the future if Pine Creek Farm became their permanent home. "I think you should ask him that first thing tomorrow."

Chapter Fourteen

Holt loaded two fishing poles into the bed of his truck and shut the tailgate. "I think that'll do it."

Liam, reaching into the bed of the truck and checking that everything was secure, nodded. "I'd say so. Mom packed at least a dozen pimento sandwiches in the cooler and two dozen bottles of water. I'd say you're set for two days at the pond, at least."

Holt laughed. "She can't stand to see anyone go hungry. You sure you don't want to come with us? We could have a good old-fashioned competition like we used to."

Liam smiled. "Nah, I'll let y'all have it today. There's a lot I need to catch up on around here. The boys will have a blast. You couldn't have picked a better morning for fishing. Bet they'll be biting up a storm at the pond."

Holt tilted his head back and inhaled. Fresh morning air rushed in, filling his lungs and lifting his spirit. He closed his eyes and lingered in the moment, the scent of honeysuckle surrounding him. He was about to take his sons fishing—and not just anywhere, but he was taking them fishing at the pond of his childhood home.

The thought should've been exhilarating. Should've rushed over him in an intense wave of gratitude. But the unsettled feeling from yesterday still lingered within him, creating a hollow in his heart, which should be otherwise full if not overflowing.

Despite the success of the visit home thus far, he couldn't help but think something wasn't quite right.

"Good morning."

At the sound of Jessie's voice, he smiled and opened his eyes. There she was, walking across the front lawn with Cody and Devin on either side of her, holding their hands, her auburn hair cascading over her shoulders. Morning sunlight peeked over the hilly horizon at their backs, casting a rosy glow over them as they made their way across the grassy lawn. For some reason, the sight soothed his soul.

"Morning," Holt called back, waving. "Hope I'm not dragging y'all out of the bed too early."

Jessie shook her head as they drew close. "The boys were so excited they barely slept last night."

Releasing her hands, Cody and Devin ran across the short distance separating them from Holt and proceeded to climb onto the tailgate of the truck.

"What kind of fishing poles you got, Mr. Holt?" Cody asked, grabbing one and inspecting the clear fishing line.

"The user-friendly kind." Holt steadied Cody with a hand on his waist as the boy bent way over into the bed of the truck and lifted a blue fishing pole out of the bunch. "You see that right there?" Holt asked, pointing at the round red-and-white cork attached to the line. "That's your cork."

Cody wrinkled his nose. "Cork?"

"Yep." Holt tapped the wrinkles in his nose. "Some people call them bobbers or floats. When a fish chomps down on your bait and pulls, that little guy goes under water and that lets you know it's time to yank on that rod and reel a fish in."

Cody bounced with excitement. "I want to use this one! Can I?"

Holt laughed. "Yep. It's all yours. But for now—" he removed the fishing rod from Cody's hands and returned it to the truck bed

"—it needs to stay back here until we reach the pond."

Placing one hand on Holt's wrist, Cody jumped from the truck and ran toward the passenger door. "Then let's go! I'm ready to fish!"

Smiling, Holt looked at Devin, who was still surveying the contents of the truck bed, his expression somewhat somber for a fishing trip. "How 'bout you, Devin? What type of fish are you itching to reel in from the pond?"

Devin fiddled with the handle of a tackle box for another moment then ducked his head and climbed down off the truck bed. "A bass, I guess."

Holt watched him walk around the truck toward the driver's side, his arms hanging by his sides. "You all right this morning, Devin?"

He glanced back and shrugged. "Yeah. Just tired, I guess."

That was two *guesses* so far. Holt frowned. Maybe Devin would perk up a bit once they reached the pond.

"He had a long night," Jessie said, walking over to Holt's side. "There's something he'd like to talk to you about this morning, if you don't mind."

The expression on her face was so similar to Devin's he was hesitant to proceed until whatever situation this was could be resolved.

"Should we go back to the house?" he asked. "We could talk there and—"

"No." Jessie bit her lip as she glanced in Liam's direction, the two of them exchanging a look, then met Holt's eyes. "It's a beautiful morning. We'll take them to the pond and we can talk there."

Unease crept up his spine, but he nodded. "Okay. If you think that's best, that's what we'll do."

One hour later the sun was up, the fish were biting and Holt was having a fantastic time.

"I think I see a nibble, Cody." Holt, seated on the bank of the pond between Cody and Devin, leaned over and whispered in Cody's direction again. "Have a look at your cork."

Cody scooted a couple inches forward across the sandy dirt, his eyes fixated on the red-and-white cork in the distance. "You sure?" he whispered back. "I didn't notice noth—"

Devin gasped. "Right there." He reached across Holt and pointed toward Cody's cork, bouncing his legs when the cork bobbed deeper below the water. "There it goes again, Cody."

"I see it!" Cody sprang to his feet and jerked his fishing pole upright, squealing when it pulled tight against him. "I got him! I got him!" He bounced up and down, his fishing rod almost falling from his hands. "Do you see I got him, Mr. Holt?"

Laughing, Holt placed his fishing pole on the ground, sprang to his feet and wrapped his arms around Cody's, covering Cody's small hands with his around the pole. "You got 'em, kid. But you won't have him long if you don't keep a firm hold on this pole."

"Pull him!" Devin shouted as he jumped to his feet, grabbed Cody's fishing pole and started yanking, too. "Pull him in, Cody!"

A giggle burst from Cody's lips, and he yanked harder, his small frame jerking violently against Holt's chest. "We're gonna get him, Jessie! You watch. We're gonna get him!"

A familiar laugh rang out and Holt glanced to his right. There Jessie sat as she had for the past hour, leaning back against a massive knot of roots protruding from the ground, her long, jean-clad legs stretched out in front of her. Now, instead of her flushed face tilting in the direction of the sun as it spilled across the pond, she watched the three of them wrestle a stubborn fish in deep water.

She laughed again and Holt stilled, a sense of déjà vu washing over him. He'd seen that look before on her face—that same bright smile and beautiful expression on her sun-flushed face.

He smiled as her gaze found his, their eyes meeting. Ah, the picture! The large framed portrait on the wall of her cabin, depicting her in a mountain river with the boys, all smiles. The one he'd noticed on the very first day he'd returned to her door, seeking her help in finding Cody and Devin.

Happiness. Pure and whole.

But a moment later that look was gone. Once she noticed him watching her, her smile slowly faded to a fraction of what it had been and the excited light in her eyes died. She glanced at him and the boys then looked down, her hands fidgeting nervously in her lap.

Holt frowned.

"Got it!" Cody heaved hard on his fishing pole and the line sprang free of the water, a large bass flopping through the air, its shiny scales flashing in the sunlight as Cody and Devin toppled backward, slamming into Holt's gut and knocking all three of them to the ground.

Winded, Holt closed his eyes, his smile growing wider as Cody and Devin, still piled on top of him, wriggled around, trying to get to their feet and grab hold of the bass.

"Easy, boys, easy." Jessie's sweet voice sounded above him, and the boys' extra weight rolled off him, freeing him to breathe deeply. "Holt?"

He opened his eyes and there she was, standing over him now, her long hair cascading down around her face as she stared down at him with a concerned expression.

She frowned. "Are you okay?"

He nodded just a bit, looking up at her, then at the boys tussling on the bank with the bass, wanting to hold on to the moment just a little longer. "Yeah. I'm good."

"You're great!" Cody's little body hurled back onto Holt's middle, stealing his breath. "Best fisherman ever!"

Laughing, Holt flexed his abs and pulled himself to a seated position. "Hey, easy there. Let me catch my breath."

"But look!" Cody shoved his fishing line in front of Holt's face, the bass wriggling on the end of the hook. "Look at how big he is! We could have him for dinner!"

Holt smiled. "We sure could."

"You're kinda good at this, aren't you?" Devin asked, smiling. "You catch a lot of fish when you were our age?"

Holt wrapped one arm around Cody, who still beamed at his catch and shrugged. "I caught my fair share. Liam was always right behind me, though. A lot of the biggest fish I caught, I wouldn't have snagged without his help." His chest warmed as he glanced from Devin to Cody then back. "Kind of like what you two did just now. You worked together and that made all the difference."

Devin looked at Cody, who lifted his floppy fish in the air, then he met Holt's eyes again, that somber look Holt had noticed on his face earlier that morning returning. "Can I ask you something, Mr. Holt?"

Holt nodded. "Of course. You can ask me anything."

Cody, still wriggling happily against Holt's side, suddenly froze. His eyes fixated on Holt's face, wide with expectation.

"Here," Jessie said softly as she bent between Holt and the boys and took Cody's fish and fishing rod from him. "I'll put the fish on ice in the cooler."

"Jessie?" Devin called as she walked toward the truck. "Will you stay?"

A hesitant expression crossed her face, an anxious look in her eyes as she bit her lip. "Do you want me to?"

Devin nodded. "Yes, ma'am."

"Okay," she said quietly. "Give me just a moment."

Holt frowned, his heart aching at her discomfort, wondering what had unsettled her.

He studied Devin's face, but the boy lowered his head and picked at a bit of grass between his shoelaces, hiding his expression.

Jessie returned shortly and eased onto the ground a couple feet away from Holt and the boys. She nodded encouragingly at Devin, but her mouth shook slightly. "Go ahead, Devin."

Devin looked up then, his gaze roving Holt's face as he asked, "Are you our dad?"

Holt's heart kicked against his ribs, stealing his breath. He glanced at Jessie and she seemed unsurprised, as though she'd been expecting Devin's question, but there were shadows of sadness in her eyes and her lips still trembled.

Holt supposed he should've seen this coming, too, but he'd imagined it all playing out differently. That he and Jessie would sit down and discuss the situation again, she would tell him when she was ready to inform the boys of his identity and they'd break the news to Cody and Devin gently…together.

Instead, Cody and Devin had taken the lead, put him on the spot and left him floundering for words. And Jessie seemed as though she felt all alone, sitting on the outside and looking in when instead, she held a place in his heart right alongside the boys.

He studied his sons' faces for a moment, the

hope in both of their eyes giving him courage. "Yes," he whispered. "I'm your dad."

Devin and Cody fell silent, their wide gazes moving from Holt's face to Jessie's then each other's.

Finally, Cody sighed. "Devin thought you were. He said you have a twin like us and hair like us and eyes like us and—"

Devin scowled, his chin trembling. "But why did you leave us? Didn't you want us?"

It was like a gut punch, sucking all the air out of Holt's lungs. Eyes burning, he shook his head and scooted forward across the dirt, sitting as close as he possibly could to both of them, struggling to steady the waver in his voice. "I wanted you both very much." His throat tightened. "Very, very much."

Two big tears rolled down Devin's cheeks as he stared back at Holt, his voice breaking on his next words. "But you never came to see us. You never called. Never came to our birthday parties, never took us anywhere. You didn't do any of the things the other dads do for their kids."

Holt dipped his head, wet heat coursing down his cheeks. "I know. I should've stayed with you both. I should've made better choices. I should've been braver. Stronger."

Cody, tears running down his cheeks,

dragged the back of his hand across his face and swallowed hard. "But you're brave now, aren't you? You're strong enough for us now?"

His hands shook. Holt held them out, palms up, one on each leg, keeping them steady. "Yes. I've spent a lot of time changing, becoming the father you both deserve, and I came back for you. I came back because I missed you. Because I want to be a part of your lives. And I want the chance to be your dad, if you'll have me. Because I love you."

"No, you don't." Devin's hands balled into fists as he stared at Holt's face, picking apart his expression. "Y-you can't. If you loved us, you wouldn't have left us."

"Devin." Jessie's soft voice sounded by Holt's side. She reached out and covered one of Devin's hands with her own. "Holt left you because he thought it was what was best for you at the time. He gave you to me because he knew I would take good care of you and Cody. He loved you enough to ask someone to do what he wasn't able to at the time."

Holt, choking back a sob, nodded. "I know how hard this must be for you both to believe, but I love you both more than you'll ever know."

Cody threw himself against Holt's chest, clutched the front of Holt's T-shirt and pressed his face to Holt's neck, sobs bursting from his lips as he whispered, "It's okay. I'm not mad at you," he said. "I love you, too."

Devin stared at Holt, tears coursing down his cheeks.

"I'm here now, Devin," Holt said, hugging Cody close. "Whenever you need me, I'll be here for you and I'll wait as long as it takes for you to trust me."

Devin dragged the back of his hands over his cheeks and looked at Jessie then back at Holt. "But…but you're not leaving again?"

Holt, his throat tight with emotion, shook his head.

A fresh set of tears coursed down Devin's cheeks. "You promise?"

"I promise," Holt said, holding out his hand.

Devin stared at it for a moment then looked at Jessie again, a question in his eyes.

Jessie nodded. "It's okay to give him a chance if you'd like to," she whispered.

At her reassurance, Devin threw himself against Holt, wrapping his arms around Holt's neck and pressing himself as close to Holt's chest as possible. They cried together, Holt closing his eyes and hugging them tightly, their tears and heartbeats mingling with his own as he silently thanked God for giving him this moment. This chance. This reality.

His chest felt fit to burst and it was hard to believe this much happiness could swell inside it, could consume his entire being so intensely without his body breaking.

Joy billowed through him in waves, and he opened his eyes and mouth to look at Jessie and call out to her, to share this moment, to thank her for giving him a chance, for seeing the man he was even when he harbored his own doubts.

But she'd slipped silently away, her slender figure walking slowly across the field on the other side of the pond, the sun bright at her back.

Chapter Fifteen

Three days later, the last day of his visit home, Holt stood in the dark on the front porch of Pine Creek Farm's main house, sipping a bitter cup of coffee and staring toward the horizon.

"Couldn't sleep?" The screen door creaked as Liam walked out onto the porch and joined Holt at the railing, a steaming cup of coffee cradled in his hands, too.

Holt shook his head. "No."

Although that was nothing new. It'd been three days since he'd revealed his identity to Cody and Devin at Pine Creek's fishing hole and every night since, he'd tossed and turned, stared up at the ceiling of his bedroom, waiting for the sun to rise so he could show Cody, Devin and Jessie around the farm and put in a decent day's work. Anything to slow the thoughts tumbling in his mind and help him close his eyes at night. Only, nothing had worked.

After his conversation with Cody and Devin by the fishing hole, he and the boys spent the rest of the afternoon together, fishing, talking and laughing. Holt's heart had never felt so full...until they'd returned to the house and he'd caught a glimpse of the pained expression on Jessie's face. Rather than bringing them closer together, revealing his identity to Cody and Devin had seemed to cause Jessie to withdraw.

And later that evening, when Jessie had shared with him that she would step back for the next few days and give him and the boys space to acquaint themselves with each other better alone, his high spirits had deflated at the thought of enjoying time with Cody and Devin without her as well. He knew she was supporting his relationship with his sons and giving them time alone together, but it had only taken one subsequent fishing trip with the boys without her for him to realize how much he missed her being there with them. How much they'd begun to feel like a family. And how much he wanted to formally make them one.

Only, it wasn't the right time to tell her. Not until he'd spoken with his mom and Liam.

"It's four forty-five in the morning," Liam

murmured before taking another sip of coffee. "You gonna stand out here 'til the sun rises?"

Holt nodded. "Probably." He glanced over at Liam. "And you're one to talk. What're you doing up?"

He shrugged, his lips twitching. "Pangs of twin sympathy, I suppose. And that French roast aroma found its way into my left nostril and woke me right up."

Holt laughed.

They stood there silently for several minutes, sipping their coffee and peering into the dark, then Liam said, "Listen, you haven't had enough sleep to work today. Take the day off. Spend it here at the house with Jessie and the boys. Eat a big lunch and take a long afternoon nap before y'all hit the road later."

Holt shook his head. "I can't."

Liam fell silent and faced forward, staring out into the darkness. "And why not?"

Holt closed his eyes. Because he'd made a decision. One he was afraid might break Liam's and his mother's hearts. Though that wouldn't reverse the decision he'd made. At some point during the dark, endless hours he'd spent staring at the ceiling last night, he'd come to a realization. One that changed everything.

"Do you know," he asked Liam softly, "that ever since I came back home, I've felt as though something was missing? As though something wasn't right?"

Liam shifted beside him, and Holt could feel the weight of his gaze on him.

"I couldn't put my finger on it," Holt continued. "I couldn't figure out what was bothering me so much. And then, as soon as Cody and Devin were in my arms by the pond the other day and I looked up and saw Jessie walking away, I knew exactly what it was."

Liam remained silent.

Holt stared ahead into the darkness, peering into the distance, trying to find the horizon. "Pine Creek doesn't feel like home to me anymore." He glanced at Liam hesitantly, unsure of how he'd respond. "I don't want to offend you or Mom, but I want to be honest with you."

"I know." Liam sipped his coffee again then asked, "Where *do* you feel at home?"

An image of Creek Cabin rose to Holt's mind. He could almost smell the fresh wood on the back deck and charcoal smoldering in the grill. He could hear Cody, Devin and Miles' cheerful chatter during snack time in the community cabin. Feel the warm spring breeze on his face and see Jessie's auburn hair swinging softly along her back as she led the way along a dirt trail winding through a thick line of trees. And he could still feel baby Ava's slight weight in his arms, see her wide eyes and bright smile and hear her cheerful babble.

"Hummingbird Haven," he whispered. "With Jessie, Cody and Devin, and with Ava nearby or in my arms. That's where I feel most at home."

Confusion filled Liam's eyes. "Who's Ava?"

Holt smiled. "A baby girl with the biggest blue eyes I've ever seen who helped me reacquaint myself with the man I really am." He looked at Liam, an earnest tone entering his voice. "I didn't end up on Jessie's doorstep with Cody and Devin by accident seven years ago. I was led there by word of mouth and something more." He touched his chest, his palm covering the spot where his heartbeat pulsed against his skin. "I felt it here. Something called to me, led me to Jessie back then. I felt it again when I returned to her cabin a couple months ago. When I knocked on her door, summoning up the courage to ask her to help me find Cody and Devin."

Holt stopped and looked out across the grounds again, the corners of his mouth tipping up as a faint glow peeked just a smidge over the horizon. "And I feel it again now— ever since I arrived here. I feel a pull to take a different path. To be something more. To make a difference in others' lives." He looked at Liam and smiled, the proud gleam in his brother's eyes urging him to continue. "I'm being called to a new purpose. The same one as Jessie. I've never felt more valuable or worthy as I did when I worked with her and the residents at Hummingbird Haven these past weeks. When I helped Ava feel safe in my arms and helped Peggy Ann smile. When I helped Miles find his confidence—enough so, that he was willing to try new things and discover he was stronger than he ever knew."

Liam smiled. "Sounds like you've already made up your mind about what you want to do."

"I have. And I hope it's what Jessie wants, too. I want her, Cody and Devin to be in my life every day." Holt winced. "But I don't want to disappoint you or Mom. You both waited so long for me to come back and as soon as business is thriving and things are going well, here I am wanting to leave again…and take my sons with me."

The porch door creaked again, and a feminine voice asked softly, "Do you love her?"

Holt spun around, surprised to see his mother standing there in her fuzzy bathrobe and slippers, a tremulous smile on her face.

"Are you doing this for you and not just for the boys?" she asked.

"Yes," he whispered. "I love Jessie as much as I love my sons. I've never forgotten her over the years, and I can't imagine my life without her now."

Gayle lifted her chin and nodded. "Then your home is with her."

Holt walked across the porch to her side and took her hands in his. "I don't want to leave you like D—"

"Oh, I'll have none of that." Gayle waved away his words with one hand then pulled him close for a tight hug. "You're nothing like your father, Holt," she whispered in his ear. "You're a good, strong, loyal man who will be an excellent dad. And I'm so glad you've found your way." She released him and stepped back, cupping his cheek with one hand. "You don't need my permission to begin a new life with Jessie and the boys at Hummingbird Haven," she said softly, "but you have my blessing."

Smiling so hard his cheeks hurt, Holt hugged her tight then hugged Liam and slapped his back for good measure. He took off down the front porch steps and across the lawn, tugging his cell phone from his back pocket and lifting his face toward the first tendrils of morning sunlight as they reached just above the horizon and brightened the sky to a spectacular blend of pink, lavender and gold.

"What are you doing?" Liam called from the front porch.

"Gotta make a call." Holt kept walking and smiling as he dialed then brought the phone to his ear and waited for a familiar voice to answer.

"Hope Springs Hospital. This is Sharon James. How may I assist you?"

Jessie, seated at a table in Hummingbird Haven's community cabin, poked at the salad on her plate twice then laid her fork down.

"Lettuce is good for you, Jessie. Zoe says it's roughage and helps clean out your system."

She looked across the table at Miles, who studied her closely, his plate empty, and smiled as Zoe, sitting beside him, tsked her tongue.

"I know I said that, Miles," Zoe said, "but it's not exactly the best topic to bring up at the table."

Jessie laughed. "It's okay. You're absolutely right, Miles, and normally, I'd eat this salad right up. I'm just not feeling well today. That's all."

Miles perked up. "Then can I have your salad? The rest is already gone and I'm still hungry."

Jessie glanced at the large salad bowl she'd placed on the table an hour earlier and it was indeed empty…as should be expected.

Spring break at Hummingbird Haven had always been a busy, energetic time for everyone what with the kids out of school for the week with tons of free time and wonderful weather. And after returning from Pine Creek yesterday, she'd filled the last day of vacation with extra loads of laundry, meal preps and coordinating outdoor activities. Only, something was missing. Three somethings, to be precise.

"Have at it." Jessie nudged her salad plate across the table to Miles, watching as he dug into it with gusto.

She looked to her left down the table where Peggy Ann's daughters, Tabitha and Katie, played a round of Crazy Eights, their tenth competition, Jessie guessed, and chatted about different techniques of braiding hair. Glancing to her right, she noticed Zoe staring back at her, a question in her eyes.

"Please don't look at me like that," Jessie said quietly, casting a quick glance at Miles, who continued munching happily on her salad.

Zoe blinked, striving valiantly for a bewildered expression. "What do you mean? What look?"

Jessie pointed at her face. "That look. The one you make when you're covering up the other look I don't like."

Zoe frowned. "Which one is that?"

"The pity one." Sighing, Jessie rubbed her forehead. "The one you've given me way too often the past twenty-four hours when you think I won't notice."

Zoe slumped back in her seat, disappointment in her eyes. "Really? I thought I was hiding it better than that and I assure you, I've been trying very hard."

And she had been. Ever since Jessie had returned home, told Zoe the boys knew Holt was their father then expressed her fears over what the future may hold, Zoe had worked extremely hard to simultaneously cheer her up and keep an inconspicuous but concerned eye on her. Zoe was a good friend—the best, really—and Jessie loved her all the more for her attempts to ease her concerns.

Unfortunately, the kind of worries she carried weren't easily assuaged. She was glad Cody and Devin knew Holt was their father, and even happier they'd begun showing a greater interest in him the last three days at Pine Creek Farm—an interest that had only continued to grow since their return to Hummingbird Haven. Even now, they were out with Holt again, either hiking mountain trails or fishing in one of the creeks behind the cabins.

She was glad they were spending time together, but it was an odd, unwelcome feeling to sit in an empty cabin without the boys. A feeling she wasn't sure she would ever get used to but would have to at some point now that she and Holt would be sharing custody of the boys.

Jessie stood and headed for the door.

Zoe called after her. "Where are you going?"

She paused in the doorway and summoned a small smile. "I still have more cleaning to do. Would you mind watching the kids while I work on it?"

Zoe smiled back but concern still lingered in her eyes. "Not at all. I'm taking them on a hike down a new trail later anyway. We'll be passing by your cabin. I'll stop by on the way and if you feel up to it, you're welcome to join us."

"I'll think about it," Jessie said.

And she would...think about it, that was. Because she knew that in the end, she wouldn't go. It was just too hard to be around the kids more than she needed to right now. Their very presence reminded her of Cody and Devin's absence...as well as Holt's, and that soon, Holt would probably approach her with the request to take Cody and Devin home with him to Pine Creek Farm. She would agree because it was the right thing to do and all three of them would be missing from her daily life more often than not.

She walked to her cabin and swept the kitchen floor and polished the hardwood floors in the living room. She dusted the lamps and changed the sheets on her bed then returned to the kitchen and stood by the island idly for a few minutes, rubbing her middle right where a hollowness had settled ever since Holt and the boys had left early that morning.

Staying busy didn't ease it but standing still didn't seem to help, either.

Shaking her head, she lifted her chin and forced a smile instead. "They're happy," she reminded herself. "I should be happy because they're happy and that's exactly what I'm going to be."

She meant it, every word. But she didn't quite feel it as she looked around at the empty cabin.

A knock sounded at the front door and she crossed the room and opened it. "I'm sorry, Zoe. I'm not feeling like a hike tod—"

Her words trailed away, her voice failing her as she saw the man standing on the other side of the door.

"Holt." She stared at him, her gaze lingering on the tender look in his eyes, the strong curve of his jaw, the bright smile curling his lips and...*the pink bundle in his strong arms?* "You—you have another one?"

His smile widened as he looked down at her, a chuckle rumbling through his wide chest.

"I—I mean…" Heat burned up her neck and suffused her cheeks. "Of course I know you didn't have another baby. I just meant you brought another one to me." She shoved her hair away from her hot face. "Is—is that Ava?"

He removed one big hand from beneath the pink bundle and drew back the blanket, revealing the baby's face. Ava's big blue eyes met hers and the baby smiled, kicking her legs and waving her tiny fists in the air with gleeful recognition.

"She's missed us both while we were away this week," Holt said. "So I thought we'd stop by and visit on the way to my cabin."

"Your cabin?" Jessie shook her head. "What do you mean, your cabin? I thought you and the boys—"

"The boys and I had a long talk this morning," he said softly. "I shared a few of my plans with them and they liked the sound of them." He turned to the side and spoke over his shoulder. "You can come on up now, boys."

Footsteps scrambled up the front steps as Holt shifted to the side, revealing Cody and Devin dashing toward her, huge smiles on both their faces. They barreled into her, throwing their arms around her waist and pressing their cheeks to her middle.

"We're gonna have a sister, Jessie!" Devin shouted.

"And Dad's gonna work on one of the cabins so we can all stay in the same house together," Cody said, bouncing against her.

Jessie, hugging them close and kissing their blond heads, stilled and looked up at Holt in surprise. "Holt, what're they talking about?"

"Boys." Holt waited as Cody and Devin released her and looked up at him. "Do you remember how I showed you how to hold Ava on your lap earlier?"

Devin nodded, a solemn look in his eyes. "Always support her head."

Holt smiled. "That's right. Why don't you have a seat on the couch over there and hold her for a minute while I talk to your mom?"

Jessie's mouth parted, her breath pausing as Cody and Devin smiled up at her then skipped over to the couch and sat down beside each other, keeping still as Holt lowered Ava carefully onto Devin's lap, then waiting patiently as he took care to make a safe little nest of pillows to ensure she was safe and secure in Devin's arms.

"Stay right there and don't move 'til we come back, okay?" Holt asked.

Devin and Cody answered in unison. "Yes, sir."

Beaming with pride, Holt cupped his hand under Jessie's elbow and tugged her out onto the porch. "There's something I want to ask you."

Jessie gripped his forearms and stared up at him, almost unable to believe he stood in front of her. "What's going on, Holt? A cabin for all of us to stay in together?"

A slow smile lifted his tempting lips. "Well, that depends."

Her pounding heart slowed a bit. "On what?"

"On how long it takes me to renovate Hummingbird Hollow and add an extra room suitable for a nursery."

Her pulse picked up again. "A-a nursery?"

His smile widened. "Yeah. Ava's going to need her own room when she gets older. We can't expect her to share with Cody and Devin."

Feeling dumb, but unable to do anything other than repeat his sentences, she dipped her head and asked, "Ava? And Cody and Devin?"

"And it'll depend on your answer." He lifted his hand and cradled her cheek, his thumb smoothing across her temple as he spoke. "I love you, Jessie." He stepped closer, his thighs brushing hers. "I want to marry you. I want to hold you in my arms every night and kiss you every morning. I want to raise our sons—and daughter—together. To give them—and whoever else God sends us—the same loving home and family that I've found here with you."

She smiled, unable to stop the tears flowing down her cheeks. "Y-you love me?"

He nodded, certainty in his gaze. "And I'm hoping you love me, too. I no longer have any doubts—not about who I am or my ability to be a good father, and certainly not about my love for you. I have faith in us, and I know you have faith in me. And the two of us, together—our love and our new family—would be the best haven my sons could ever have." He lowered his head, his eyes searching hers. "Please say yes," he whispered. "Say you'll marry me. Say you lo—"

She did better. She showed him.

She rose up to her tiptoes and her lips met his, her palms cupping his face as she kissed him, breathing him in, savoring the feel of his mouth against hers, his strong arms around her, his chest vibrating gently against hers on a low groan.

Lifting his head, he drew in a ragged breath, his eyes darkening as he smiled wide and looked down at her. "I'll take that as a yes," he whispered.

Jessie smiled back. "Yes. I love you." She traced the curve of his cheek lovingly. "And I'd be honored to be your wife."

He lowered his head and kissed her once more, slowly and tenderly, then took her hand and led her inside the cabin where Cody, Devin, Ava…and a future full of love awaited them.

* * * * *

Get 3 FREE REWARDS!

We'll send you 2 FREE Books plus a FREE Mystery Gift.

FREE Value Over **$20**

Both the **Harlequin® Special Edition** and **Harlequin® Heartwarming™** series feature compelling novels filled with stories of love and strength where the bonds of friendship, family and community unite.

CARING FOR HER AMISH NEIGHBOR
Amish of Prince Edward Island • by Jo Ann Brown

When an accident leaves Juan Kuepfer blind, widow Annalise Overgard and her daughter, who is visually impaired, are the only ones who can help. He needs to learn how to live without his sight, but being around them brings up guilt and grief from the past. Together can they find forgiveness and happiness?

HER HIDDEN AMISH CHILD
Secret Amish Babies • by Leigh Bale

Josiah Brenneman was heartbroken when his betrothed left town without a word. Now Faith Mast is back to sell her aunt's farm—with a *kind* in tow—and Josiah has questions. Why did she leave? Can he trust that she won't run away again? And who is the father of her child?

TO PROTECT HIS BROTHER'S BABY
Sundown Valley • by Linda Goodnight

Pregnant with nowhere to go, Taylor Matheson takes refuge at her late husband's ranch. Then Wilder Littlefield shows up, claiming the ranch is his. He can't evict his brother's widow, so she can stay until the baby arrives—but soon they start to feel like family...

THE COWBOY BARGAIN
Lazy M Ranch • by Tina Radcliffe

When Sam Morgan returns home from a business trip, he's stunned to discover his grandfather has rented the building Sam wanted to his former fiancée, Olivia Moretti. He's determined to keep his distance from the woman who broke his heart, but an Oklahoma twister changes his plans...

A FAMILY TO FOSTER
by Laurel Blount

Single dad Patrick Callahan will do anything to help the foster kids in his care—including saving Hope Center, a local spot for children from disadvantaged backgrounds. When his ex-fiancée, Torey Bryant, is named codirector by her matchmaking mom, it could spell disaster...or a second chance at love.

A FATHER FOR HER BOYS
by Danielle Grandinetti

Juggling a broken foot and guardianship of her nephews, Sofia Russo gladly takes a summer house-sitting gig out in the country. When they arrive, her boys are immediately taken with local landscaper Nathaniel Turner. And she can't help but feel something too. Could he be what they've been missing all along?

LICNM0723

HARLEQUIN
PLUS

Try the best multimedia subscription service for romance readers like you!

Read, Watch and Play.

Experience the easiest way to get the romance content you crave.

Start your **FREE TRIAL** at
www.harlequinplus.com/freetrial.